THE D
RO

By
Gerald A. Moriarty

Strategic Book Publishing and Rights Co.

Strategic Book Publishing and Rights Co., LLC
USA | Singapore
www.sbpra.net

For information about special discounts for bulk purchases, please contact Strategic Book Publishing and Rights Co., LLC. Special Sales, at bookorder@sbpra.net.

ISBN: 978-1-949483-90-1

Other books by the author

Beware the Gaheena!

In Search of Silver Wolf:
The sequel to Beware the Gaheena!

A Perilous Journey to Peace

Legend on the Mountain:
The legacy of Silver Wolf

Vanishing Anger

Pools of Gold:
A Sequel to Vanishing Anger

Dedication

I dedicate this book to my family physician, Dr. Randy Magley, MD, and his wife, Pat. I can truthfully credit Randy with saving my life. He is gifted with the uncanny ability to see beyond the immediate. He and his family are perfect examples for all to follow. I first met this family high up in the back country of the Cascade Mountains east of Enumclaw, Washington.

Preface

Randy leaves his comfortable home in Gila Bend, which is located just south of what's been called the Great Grand Canyons of the Arizona Territory and heads out to seek a wilder way of life than the one he has been living. He gets what he is looking for and much more than he had bargained for. He ends up on the run from the law and just about everybody he has ever came in contact with. In the end, he is severely wounded, seeking shelter and help. His life takes a drastic change when help arrives. He was a lucky man to have lived and survived his past.

Chapter One

A young man by the name of Randy Dawkins, who had been raised in a small settlement by the name of Gila Bend, decided it wasn't wild enough for him there. He packed his gear onto his horse and rode out of the settlement, raising all kinds of hell as he did. He wanted to make his own fame. As it turns out, he went well beyond what he had intended. As he made his way around the territory, he stopped in every settlement he came to that had a saloon. In each place he stopped, it wasn't long before he was escorted to the edge of the settlement and told not to look back. He cheated at cards and pounded on a few heads, leaving more than a few under a doctor's care.

In one card game, he won a horse that was beyond anyone's dreams. The horse was so fast taking off that one had to hold tight to the saddle horn to keep from being flipped over the back of the saddle. Its speed was envied by all who desired a fast horse. It had never been beaten in a race by another horse. Many tried, but none could get the job done. Its reputation became so well known that nobody challenged it again. The owner never gave the horse its full reign, so its full potential had never been discovered. Randy soon found out what that potential was, as he needed that speed more than ever before.

It was in one of these settlements that his notoriety became the talk of the territory and continued throughout the entire wild west. He became a feared man, even to his peers. He had been tagged with the name of Wild Man Randy. Some called him, The Man from Hell. He became extremely fast on the draw and accurate with his aim. He also was extremely ruthless in his manner. It was at the settlement of Gallup that he decided the measly sum he swindled out of the players at the card tables wasn't enough.

In another card game he joined, he shot and killed a notorious gunslinger who had called him out for cheating. The gunslinger had the reputation of being the fastest draw in the land. Absolutely no one could believe what they had just witnessed. Randy wasn't satisfied with just picking up his winnings— he took the gunslinger's as well as all the other players' money. Once again he was escorted to the edge of the settlement and told not to look back. As he turned to ride away, they thanked him for ridding the settlement of that scum. They just didn't want him to hang around and replace the gunslinger. That would only invite more like him to settle around their usually quiet settlement.

Randy's lightning speed with his draw, which enabled him to kill that famous gunslinger, became the word of the territory. Because of that, he became the most sought after quick draw that every fast gun throughout the Wild West wanted to challenge. He constantly had to be on the move, and he had to be watching his back at all times.

His home was in the wild lands with the animals, snakes, and Indians. Wild Man Randy had bit off more than he had intended to chew. His fame had kept him from being able to partake in many of the saloons he so enjoyed. His money drained away as time passed, and he made the mistake of his life when he decided to rob a stagecoach serving the territory.

During the course of relieving the passengers of their money and jewelry, one of the passengers recognized him and was about to yell out his name, so Wild Man Randy shot him to shut him up. As the man lay dying, he gasped out the name "Randy" before succumbing to that fatal shot. When the stagecoach reached the next settlement, the name *Randy* spread as the name of the man who had robbed the coach. It didn't take long until those who heard about it put two and two together and identified the killer as Wild Man Randy. Randy now needed a hiding place that would give him relief from being constantly sought after. He was weary and severely needed sleep.

One day, while he was trying to escape those who sought him, he rode up into steep hillside country that was covered with large boulders and brush. He reigned up behind one of the brush's outcroppings and dismounted. His pursuers had passed by and, in the end, finally gave up the chase. Randy began looking around the terrain behind the brush outcropping for a place to make camp.

The ground dropped off at a steep rate. Randy noticed an animal trail winding its way down the hillside behind all that brush. He followed the trail to the bottom where the trail took a sharp turn into what appeared to be an opening in the hillside. It turned out to be exactly what he was looking for—a hideout. A large outcrop overhung a wide opening, which allowed him to set up camp with plenty of room for his horse and belongings. He would be able to stay dry even during the worst of storms. The way he rode in behind the brush was perfect for escaping his pursuers, undetected. It was all rock, so no tracks would be left for anybody to follow. His horse was so fast anyway, that he would be out of sight shortly after any chase began.

Water had always been a problem until, on one of his excursions, he found a small spring about a half mile from his camp. It formed from the bottom of a small pool, and then evaporated away before it reached any place that it might be detected. It was a surprise to him to see there was no sign that it had ever been detected before. He sprinkled dust around the area to make it impossible for anyone else to access the spring without leaving tracks. He would always brush out his own tracks while leaving the area.

Randy soon realized that he needed a safe place to obtain his needed supplies. A settlement was located to the northwest of his hideout, a settlement he had not yet explored. It always seemed to be too far out of the way to bother with. However, he planned his next outing for that settlement. It would be a full day's ride, beginning at dawn and ending at dark. He decided he would have to make his camp out and away from the settlement, just in case someone there might recognize him.

He made the decision to stay away from any saloon, as he didn't want to be tempted to enter any card game, which always caused him to have to leave in a hurry . . . escorted.

His food supply and coffee had been depleted for several days now. All he had left were some small pieces of jerky. His hunger was getting the best of him. He had been in his hideout long enough that he felt it would be safe now to travel to the settlement for supplies. He decided to leave at first light the next morning. He filled his water pouch from the spring and carried enough back to his camp to be sure his horse would be well-watered for the long day's ride. He placed what little of the jerky he had left into his saddle bag.

Chapter Two

Morning came early for Randy Dawkins, as he was excited about leaving his hideout for the first time since being pursued by that angry bunch who wanted to hang him. He knew it wouldn't be a trouble-free ride, as he had been told of two nomadic tribes that were extremely hostile. He would have to watch out for them at all times.

He carefully made his way out of his hideout and stopped short at the end of the brush that hid him. He looked the area over for a few minutes before emerging out into the open. He headed in a westerly direction until he had cleared the rocky hillside in which he had been hiding. He then urged his horse in a northerly direction.

The morning was clear, and the sun began to heat the air and ground. It was becoming miserably hot. He wanted to find a place to escape the sun for a time, but his stomach overruled him. He had been on the trail for somewhere around four hours when he stumbled upon a spring.

He dismounted, and then bent down by the spring and began tossing water all over

Gerald A. Moriarty

himself. The water was cold. The spring was small. If it had been large enough, he would have sat in it. He took a long drink, and then led his horse to the edge of the spring so it could satisfy its thirst. Once the horse was satisfied, Randy threw water over it as well. He could see his horse really liked that.

Randy bent down by the spring and once again tossed water all over himself. He then mounted up and headed towards where he thought the settlement was located. After another hour of riding, he spotted smoke rising in the distance. He guided his horse towards the smoke, which was pretty much in the same direction he was headed anyway.

When he arrived to a place that he could determine where the smoke was coming from, he saw several buildings burned to the ground, but still smoldering. He rode toward them to see what was going on, and when he arrived, he wished he hadn't. There were two women and three children lying on the ground, scattered all over the place—they had been scalped and disemboweled. It was a sickening sight.

He called out to see if anyone had escaped the massacre. When he was satisfied that none had, he dismounted and looked over the dead. There appeared to be an elderly woman and perhaps the mother of the three children. The massacre had evidently happened around daybreak. What puzzled Randy was that there was no body of a man or any men of the ranch.

Randy looked around to see if there might be a tool of some sort lying around so he could dig graves for the victims. In an area that looked like it might have been a garden, he spotted what looked like a shovel. He went over and was quite relieved to see that it was what he thought it was. He picked up the shovel and began looking for a place to dig the graves and soon found an area that had soft ground. He began digging.

One by one, he brought the bodies over to their grave and gently placed them in it. He looked around until he found some cloth, and then placed it over their faces. He then filled each grave, being careful with each shovel full of dirt. He had never been to a funeral before, nor had he ever seen anyone buried. He really had no idea whether he was doing the proper thing with each of the deceased.

Randy had heard someone once say that he had said a few words over the grave after he buried someone, so he stood by the side of the graves and said that he sure hoped they made it to the happy hunting grounds and to make each shot count. After making sure he had missed no one, he mounted up and headed towards the settlement again.

After another couple of hours had passed, he spotted a lone rider coming directly towards him. Randy moved his horse to a position where he would have an unobstructed shot if he needed it, and then he stopped. He waited for the rider to get within earshot. When the rider neared him, Randy reached down and removed the safety thong from the hammer on his sidearm.

The rider called out howdy to him. Randy answered him in the same manner and asked him if he was the owner of the ranch to the south of them. The man said he was. Randy told him the bad news about what the Indians had done to his ranch and family. He told the man that he had given them all a decent burial. The rancher was totally devastated. He thanked Randy, and then whipped his horse into a run towards his ranch.

Randy just sat there and watched the man until he was well out of sight. He reset the safety thong on his sidearm, and then wheeled his horse around and headed in the direction from which the man had come. He assumed the man had come from the same settlement to which he was headed. Randy had a sick feeling in his stomach from all he had just endured.

The sun was beginning to set, and it was on the darker side of dusk when he spotted the settlement off in the distance. He rode well on into the darkness to a point just outside of the settlement and set up camp for the night. His stomach would just have to wait until morning.

Sleep was hard to come by, as all he could think about was what that rancher must be going through now. Randy caught himself with tears welling up in his eyes. He just wiped them away and rolled over in an attempt to go to sleep.

Chapter Three

Randy awoke to the noise of wagons rolling into the settlement. He rolled out of his bedroll and, without hesitation, got right to work getting his horse saddled and bedroll strapped on. He checked to make sure he had left nothing behind. All he had was his horse, saddle, bridle, bed role, a pocket full of money, and the jewelry he had taken from those on the stagecoach. He also had a belly full of hurt and growling for something to fill it. He mounted up and rode on into the settlement.

The only thing open was the livery and the eatery. He figured the eatery took priority over the livery so tied his horse up to the rail, stepped on up onto the boardwalk, and entered the eatery. He no more than sat down when a waitress came over to his table and asked him what he wanted. He told her whatever was fastest and a lot of coffee. She walked off laughing.

She had no more than walked through the batwing doors to the kitchen when she re-appeared carrying a plate heaped with food, a large pot of coffee, and a mug hanging from one finger. She chuckled as she placed it in front of him. With a wry grin on her face, she asked him if that was fast enough. He answered with his mouth full of food. She walked off laughing again, saying the answer must have been a yes.

When he finished with his food and had all the coffee he desired, he rose to leave. He placed more than enough money on the table to take care of the bill as well as an extremely large tip. The waitress walked up to him and said thanks. He asked her if there was a chance she could fix him a large bag of biscuits. She told him it would take some time to have them ready. He told her that he had to go to the livery and mercantile to supply up. She said she would have it ready for him when he got back. He thanked her, and then left.

As Randy approached the livery, he heard the sound of an anvil ringing inside the building. He rode on around to where the door was and dismounted. The blacksmith spotted him and wandered on out to him. He asked Randy what his needs were, and Randy told him to replace all the shoes on his horse and, when done with that, to fill the two bags with grain. He then told the man to remove all the gear, and then place the horse in a box stall with a small bait of grain and a manger full of hay until he got back.

Randy then headed for the mercantile, which was now open. It didn't take him long to find out that he was going to have to buy another horse to carry all the items back to his hideout. Once he had all the items he needed, he placed them by the door and told the clerk he would be back shortly to pick it all up. He then headed back to the livery.

After arriving, he asked the blacksmith if he knew of any horses around for sale. The blacksmith told Randy of one that a man had that was pretty old but still able to carry a small load. The blacksmith said he would try to round up the man and tell him of his interest in the horse. Randy told the blacksmith that he was going over to the eatery for a bite and some coffee and would be back when done.

When Randy arrived back at the livery with his bag of biscuits, the blacksmith and a broken-down old cowboy came up to him. They were leading a horse. The blacksmith introduced the two and went back to his anvil. The old cowboy told Randy that this was the horse he wanted to part with. Randy looked the horse over pretty good and came to the conclusion that the horse was indeed pretty old but, for his age, he was holding up pretty good.

Randy asked the old cowboy how much he wanted for the horse, and the old cowboy told him a hundred would get the horse for him. Randy thanked him and said it was more than he would pay for a horse that old and began to walk away. The old cowboy stopped Randy and asked him how much he would give for the horse. Randy didn't hesitate and said fifty would be more than enough. After a few minutes of the old cowboy standing there without saying anything, Randy turned to leave.

The old cowboy yelled out and asked if he would give him seventy five for the horse. Randy turned towards the old cowboy and told him he would give him sixty dollars and no more. He then told the old cowboy that it was his final offer and turned once again to leave. The old cowboy yelled back saying he would take sixty. Together they led the horse back to the blacksmith and asked for a piece of paper and a writin' stick. After getting the bill of sale taken care of, Randy handed the old cowboy sixty dollars and bid him goodbye.

Randy asked the blacksmith to check the hoofs and shoes on the horse and the blacksmith told him that he had recently put new shoes on the animal. Randy then asked the blacksmith if he had a packboard that he could acquire. The blacksmith did, and Randy placed the packboard on the horse and loaded the two sacks of grain on them, and then saddled up his own mount. He then settled up with the blacksmith.

As Randy mounted, up the blacksmith told him that it was a fine job of bartering he had done for the horse. Randy just winked at the blacksmith and rode off towards the mercantile, leading the packhorse. When he arrived at the mercantile he retrieved the two bags of supplies and placed them on the pack frame with the grain. He again mounted up and rode over to the eatery and filled his belly for the long ride back to his hideout.

Chapter Four

As Randy was about to get up to leave, he mentioned to the waitress that he wasn't looking forward to riding back past the ranch where the slaughter had taken place. The waitress asked him where the ranch was located. She was beyond shock after he told her. Her eyes filled with tears immediately. She asked how he had met the rancher. He told her that they met up while he was on his way here and had told him what had happened. The waitress asked Randy what the rancher looked like. After describing the man, the waitress yelled over to several other ranchers and told them that they had better hear this.

As they gathered around, she told them what Randy had just related to her. The one rancher just shook his head and said that it was sure enough Carl Jenkins. He turned to the others and told them that he was going down there and see what he could do to help out. All the others said for him to wait up as they were riding with him. In all, there were seven other ranchers that had met up with Randy just outside of the settlement. They were all well-armed and angry as hell. All had their bedrolls and supplies along with them.

A cry came from one of the ranchers for them to ride. In unison they rode off towards the ranch. They soon arrived at the ranch and were furious to find the rancher lying on the ground beside the graves of his family. He had committed suicide. One of the ranchers exclaimed that they needed to rid the threat of that tribe of butchers once and for all. They all agreed. They thanked Randy and went about burying the rancher with his family. There wasn't a dry eye among them.

One of the ranchers stood by the graves and spoke words of sorrow and how they would get revenge for the family. They all mounted up and were about to ride off when one of them saw that Randy was heading out with them. They stopped and told Randy that he needn't go with them as it wasn't his fight. Randy just shrugged his shoulders and said that he didn't have anything better to do, and then spurred his horse on towards where the Indians had ridden.

The tracks were clear, so it was easy to follow them. As they were about to ride up over a small knoll, one of the ranchers held up his hand for them to stop. He signaled for them all to keep quiet. He dismounted and crawled up to a bush at the crest and peeked through it for a time. He backed down away from the crest, and when he was in the middle of all of them, he said that there was somewhere around thirty to forty Indians there.

Randy told them that they had better split up into two groups of four and attack simultaneously. One of the ranchers balked saying they would all get slaughtered as they rode in. Randy said that he was going in with them or without them. The two groups split up and, at the signal, charged screaming their heads off as they fired and rode straight through the middle of the Indian camp.

The surprise of the attack shocked the tribe just long enough for all the ranchers, along with Randy, to have enough time to put nearly all of the tribe on the ground. The Indians who were left ran off towards the bushes. Randy and another rancher rode after them and, one by one, they picked off the escaping Indians until none was left. Once the ranchers were assured that all the Indians were dead, they gathered together. Randy retrieved his packhorse and rejoined the ranchers.

Randy told them that if they would like, he would be mighty proud to sit down with them over some coffee and a bite or two. They all agreed to join him. They rode around to the other side of the knoll and made a fire. The coffee was soon over the flames, and a quick meal of warmed biscuits and jerky was ready as the coffee had completed its boiling. Not much was said until they all settled back to enjoy the coffee.

The oldest rancher spoke his appreciation for Randy's leadership in taking them into the battle with the tribe. He said that without it, surely some of them would have been killed. Randy just said that it was something that had to be done. They all told Randy that if he ever needed anything to make sure to come see them. Randy said that he would remember that. He stood up, and then packed his gear. He mounted up to leave. One by one, the ranchers came over and shook his hand.

He rode off towards the south, turning to wave as he left. They all stood there waving as well. It was a long hot ride until dark overcame him, so he made a small camp and turned in for the night without eating. It had been a rough couple of days, and sleep came fast and hard. It was a clear calm night, and Randy really needed the rest. He had been through more excitement than he had bargained for.

The hot sun burning down on him woke him up. He was sweating profusely. It didn't take long before he had retrieved the water canteen and was gulping down the water. He sat in the shade of his horse while he ate a biscuit and some jerky. Even though he desired coffee, he went without it. He loaded up his supplies on the pack horse, and then saddled his mount for the remaining ride to his hideout.

The ride back to his hideout had been uneventful since leaving the ranchers. It was early afternoon when he arrived within eyesight of the area leading to his camp. He cautiously looked over the area, and once he determined it was safe to ride on in, he did. His camp had been undisturbed except for a few animals rummaging around for food, of which they found none, because there was none. Randy could have told them that. He had left there hungry, in fact.

Randy went about putting everything in its place, and then went to the spring and discovered animal tracks at its edge. They appeared to be deer tracks. A pair of them. He thought they would be a great supply of meat, easy for the taking. He filled all the water

29

containers, and then rubbed out all the tracks of himself and the deer before walking back towards his hideout, carrying the water on his overloaded back. He was now set to settle in and plan his next move.

Chapter Five

Randy spent the next few days contemplating his next excursion outside of his hideout. He began looking for an escape route in case he was compromised in this hideout. He felt that if he was trapped in this hideout, he would be waited out until he ran out of water and food. As he was looking around on the fourth day after his return, he noticed that there was a hidden tunnel through the brush that led part way up, and then around, and finally on over the top behind his hideout. It was small and would have to be opened up enough for him to squeeze through. He would have to leave everything behind, including his horses.

On the fifth day while looking around on the other side where the tunnel came out, he discovered a trail that led around to a hideout. He also discovered a spring in the middle of the brush and with plenty of feed for a horse. He felt he could set up a backup camp at that location with plenty of supplies. The problem was that he didn't know how he was going to get his horses around to it if he got trapped in his main camp.

Gerald A. Moriarty

He devised a plan where he would keep his packhorse in the backup camp. He knew his horse would come to him when he whistled. He figured he could escape to the upper camp, and then he would ride the packhorse to the end and around to the other side of the rocky outcroppings. When he got there, he would whistle and his horse would come to him on a dead run until he was within reach. They would then ride into the other hideout. There was a good escape route out of the back side of that hideout.

He felt he would need to buy another saddle for a backup. Once they were in the backup hideout, he would have time to load all his gear on the packhorse and place the other saddle on his horse and flee through that other escape route. He hoped he would never have to find out if his plan would work. But to test it out, he put the packhorse in the backup camp and tethered him near the spring. He then crawled down through the brush to his main camp and rejoined his horse. He meandered out of camp towards the spring. He looked around to make sure all was clear. It was.

He waited a short time, and then took off running down into camp and scurried into the tunnel. His horse became anxious. Once

Randy was in the other camp, he mounted the packhorse and rode to the other end of the rocky outcroppings. Once within eyesight of the area of his main camp, he let out a loud whistle. Just as he thought, his horse came on a dead run and followed him on around into his upper camp. Randy jumped off his packhorse and went over to the other one and patted him real good and gave him a handful of grain that he had stored there.

Everything had gone perfectly. Randy practiced the escape several times in the following week. It worked well each time. It was now time for him to make his way out of the hideout and on into a settlement where he could have some fun. He missed his poker games. He had heard of a settlement that was to the southwest of him that he had not yet been to, so he headed on down to it, leaving his packhorse well secured and with plenty of feed and water. When he arrived in the settlement, he spotted the saloon right off. While riding towards it, he spotted an eatery, so figured he had better eat just in case he had to leave in a hurry.

It wasn't long before he was seated at the porker table, and as usual his winnings had become quite noticeable already. One of the players mentioned that it was pretty strange that he was winning so much money so quickly. Randy reached down and took off the safety thong from his firearm. He looked the player in the eyes and asked him if he was insinuating that he was cheating.

The man had noticed that Randy had reached down under the table and figured he was ready to draw on him. He quickly stated then that, no, he wasn't thinking that at all. He just wished he was that lucky. Randy thought the man was a pretty good liar. He just chuckled and went on playing his hand. The man folded his hand and quickly left the game and the saloon. Randy could see that the other players were getting a little nervous. He quickly lost the next few hands, and then said that it was easy come, easy go. He stated that this is just how the game goes sometimes.

It seemed to settle the others down. Another man joined in the game and sat in the seat the other man had vacated. Randy told him to watch out, as the other players seemed to like giving you a little money and then taking it all back. They all let out a small chuckle. That was how the rest of the night went. A little bantering here and a little bantering there. Randy's earnings slowly built to where he felt comfortable enough to leave. He told them that it was mighty nice of them to at least leave him enough money to buy something to eat and have a soft bed to sleep in.

As he was leaving, one of the players told him to come back tomorrow and they would try and relieve him of whatever he had left. Randy just chuckled and left for the hotel. So far he had not offended anyone enough to be worried about trouble, so he booked a room for the night. He went to the mercantile and stocked up on a few more supplies. He then went to the eatery and filled up for the night. As he was leaving the eatery, he spotted a man he thought he recognized. He couldn't recall from where or when, if ever, he had seen him before.

He just shook it off and headed to his room. He ordered a hot bath. While bathing, he scrubbed his clothes clean in the tub with him. He rung them out and placed them over the back of the chairs in his room to dry. It was a hot sultry night, so he left the window open. He looked around outside the window to see if there was a way for anybody to get into his room. There wasn't. He placed the chairs in front of the window so his clothes would catch what little breeze there was coming in.

He went to bed. The thought of the man he might have recognized came back to him. He felt he really had seen the man before, but he just couldn't place where or when. He wondered if he should just ride on out of the settlement in the morning or stick around for another night. He had really enjoyed playing poker once again and had not had a problem to the extent where he would not be invited again. He rolled over and fell asleep. He woke up to the sound of horses walking past his window.

He lay there stretching out, and then rose out of bed. He went to the window and peeked out. All seemed to be in place. He took his garments and slipped them on and packed his gear. He didn't plan staying another night, as he was concerned about that face he recognized. As far as he knew, the man never saw him. He checked out and headed to the livery and retrieved his horse. He rode on over to the eatery and had breakfast.

As he was leaving the eatery, he noticed the stage coach was loading passengers, and two armed guards were loading a metal chest under the seat where the coach driver sat. There was a shotgun man sitting alongside the driver. Randy thought there must be quite a sum of money in that chest, as nervous as the two armed guards and the shotgun man were acting. He wandered over towards the coach and asked a lady standing near it where the coach was going. She told him, and he realized he knew that route well.

Chapter Six

Randy walked back to his horse and mounted up. Without hesitation, he rode on past the coach without looking at it and on out of the settlement. He deliberately rode in a direction that would take him away from the route of the coach. Once out of sight of the settlement, he spurred his horse into a dead run towards a point where he knew he could get a drop on the stagecoach.

Randy arrived at the point where he felt it was a sure bet for relieving the coach of its chest and any valuables from the rest of the passengers. Well beyond the point where he was going to stop the coach, he fell a very large tree across the wagon road. He then rode back the other way and cut another very large tree most of the way through, to the point it would take only a short time to cut completely through it when he had finished the robbery. He knew he would have time, because it would take a while for them to turn the coach around at the point of the first felled tree.

He then rode back to the place he was going to stop the coach so he could rob it. It wasn't very long before he heard the rumbling of the coach and the yells of the driver. He knew the driver would have to slow to a walk to round the corner where he had set up the trap. He braced himself for whatever might go wrong. The coach arrived, and Randy jumped out, leveling his rifle on the shotgun rider. He told them to stop.

Once the coach stopped, he ordered the shotgun rider to toss his shotgun well away from the coach. After the shotgun hit the dirt, Randy told him to slowly toss his sidearm over in the same direction. When he had, Randy ordered the driver to toss his rifle in the same place. He did. Randy then told him to do the same with his sidearm. He did. The two armed guards were riding on top with the luggage, and Randy ordered them both to shuck their weapons as well. After they complied, he then ordered them down off the other side. When they were on the ground, he told them to lay down with their belly on the ground and their hands on the back of their head. They did.

Randy then ordered the passengers out of the coach one by one where he could see their hands at all times. Three male passengers came out of the coach, and he made them strip all of their outer garments off, and they complied. He had them lie down the same way the others were. They did. Randy noticed one of the men shaking uncontrollably. He walked over to the man and placed his rifle barrel against the back of the man's head and asked him if there were any other passengers on the coach. He said if the man lied, he would blow his brain out. The man began crying and said there was one more in the coach.

Randy ordered the other man from the coach. The man slowly appeared at the door. Randy told him to keep his hands where he could see them and step down off the coach. The man did. He ordered the man to remove his outer garments. While he was doing that, Randy spotted a bulge just above the man's boot tops. He ordered the man to slowly raise his pant leg and, with two fingers, remove the firearm and toss it behind him. He complied.

Once he had all of them lined up side by side and face down with their hands on the back of their head, Randy went to the coach door and looked inside. He spotted a firearm lying on the seat. He removed the firearm and tossed it over the coach. He went back and, one by one, stripped them of their valuables and cash. He then crawled up on top of the coach and tossed the chest to the ground. He climbed back down and ordered everyone to start walking towards the front of the horses. He then ordered them to lie down as before.

Once he felt he had all of them secured, he went over to the chest and shot the lock off of it. He removed the cash from the box and placed all the jewelry and cash into his saddle bags. He then gathered all the firearms and threw them as far over the edge behind the coach as he could. He then ordered them all back into the coach. He told the driver to walk the team until he was out of sight and if he saw anybody looking back he would shoot the whole coach up. He had all the passengers facing the front.

When the coach disappeared around the bend Randy went to his horse and mounted up. He rode fast to the other tree and finished felling it across the wagon road. He then headed in a straight line for his hideout. He had to ride almost all night to arrive at his camp. Once safely tucked away, he spread his bedroll out and crawled in. He would take better care of his mount and look over his loot in the morning.

He slept well into the afternoon before he awoke. He took care of the horses, made a meal, and then sat down to see just what he had come up with. When he dumped the contents from his saddle bags, he was a little taken aback as to how good the take was. He placed all the jewelry in the bag with all the jewelry from the other robbery. He then began counting all the money. He was astonished to find that he had over ten thousand dollars. He wondered why there was so much money in that chest.

He placed all the money and jewelry back in the saddle bags, and then placed the saddle bags back onto his saddle. He then saddled his mount and loaded up some supplies. He mounted up and rode around to the other hideout. He hadn't thought about what he was doing or where he was going. He only knew he had to find a place to get rid of the jewelry and a safe environment to stow away the money. He didn't feel comfortable. Something wasn't right. He loaded all the supplies he would need for living on the trail for a long time. He rode long and hard every day in a northeast direction.

After two weeks had passed, he came to a fairly large settlement. He spotted a place with a sign hanging on the front stating the store bought and sold gold and jewelry. He approached the owner and said that his wife had passed on, and he would like to divest of all her jewelry.

He had separated all the men's jewelry from the women's. The jeweler didn't bat an eye and gave him a figure for all of it. He said it was fine jewelry and that was why he was giving him a good price for it all. He shook hands with the jeweler and pocketed the money. He went over to the mercantile and bartered with the owner over some supplies, saying he was broke and all he had were his watch and diamond ring. The owner took them. Randy felt that, if he could continue doing this at each settlement he came to, he would soon be rid of all the men's jewelry. His cash mounted up to a tidy sum.

Chapter Seven

After a week had passed, he had rid himself of all the stolen goods and was now trying to figure out what to do with all the money from the stagecoach holdup. It wouldn't be very healthy for him to be caught with it. He decided to ride northwest until he found a settlement that he could hole up in for a while, until he had the money problem solved. He made his way to a settlement that he had heard about at the previous settlement. It was located up in a territory they called Wyoming.

He was nearing the settlement when he located a small cave on a hillside. He made camp just outside of the cave. There was no room for him, but it was a great location to stash the money. He took all the gold pieces he had and stashed them in a bag along with the major portion of the cash paper he had stolen. He figured he could use some of the paper money to gamble with, and when he won, he would separate the gold coins and place them in his pocket, and then take out a small amount of paper money to gamble with some more.

The next morning, he rose early and rode on into the settlement. He spotted an eatery, so settled in for breakfast. When he was done eating, he paid with a large paper bill and received his change in gold and silver coins. He mounted up and headed over to the mercantile to supply up. Once he had that out of the way, he again paid with a large denomination paper bill and pocketed the gold and silver change. He then headed over to the livery. He had them replace the shoes on both horses and, when done, to place the animals in the corral until he returned. The liveryman had him pay up in advance for the stay in the corral as well as for the re-shoeing of the horses. He once again paid with a large bill and placed the gold and silver change in his pocket.

He went on over to the saloon for a drink and maybe a few hands of poker. He walked in through the batwing doors and slipped off to one side to let his eyes adjust to the darker interior. When his eyes had focused, he spotted a table that was empty, so seated himself. The bartender had had his eyes on him from the time he stepped into the saloon. Once he saw that Randy was seated, he yelled over and asked him which he preferred—the cheap whiskey or the good stuff. Randy told him to give him the good stuff. Once again Randy paid with a large bill. He pocketed the gold coins, but left the silver on the table to pay for another drink if he would still wanted one.

While sipping on his whisky, he looked around and spotted the poker tables, but they were all empty. He ordered another shot of whisky and, while the bartender was pouring it, Randy asked him where all the poker players were. The bartender told him that most of the players were the hired hands on the ranches scattered out across the plains and only came in to play when the weekend rolled around. He went on to say that there might be one table filled with some of the locals later on. Randy paid up, tossed the shot down, and then rose to leave, saying he might be back on the weekend.

He walked over to the stable and retrieved his horses and belongings. Once his horses were loaded, he mounted up and headed back towards his camp. He rode in behind one of the knolls, and then rode up on the backside to take a peek to see if he was being followed. It was a good habit, as sure enough he spotted a rider tracking him. He waited until the rider was about to arrive at the edge of the knoll, and then he rode on around the knoll and came up on the backside of the rider. Randy watched the rider and, sure enough, the rider stopped where Randy had swung around in back of the knoll. The rider sat there studying the area behind the knoll, looking down on the tracks from time to time.

Randy was satisfied that the rider was sure enough tracking him. He prodded his horse towards the rider, while at the same time removing the thong from his sidearm. When the rider heard Randy, he spun around, reaching for iron, only to be looking down the barrel of Randy's sidearm. Randy told the rider to slowly remove his gun belt and toss it over towards him. The rider didn't like it, but saw no other option and complied with Randy's order. Once that was settled, Randy ordered the rider to dismount and back away. The rider did.

After Randy felt he had the rider under control, he dismounted and walked towards the rider, holding his sidearm aimed on him. Randy stopped and asked the man why he was trailing him. The rider remained silent. Randy pulled back the hammer on his .44, which made a loud clicking noise. That caused the rider to open his eyes wide, and he threw his arms in the air and told Randy to hold up and he would tell him whatever he wanted to know. Randy just stood there with his best poker face on and said for him to start talking.

He began by saying the bartender ordered him to trail him. Randy asked him why. The rider said that the bartender saw the large bills he was carrying and became suspicious of him. Randy told him to mount up and head back to the settlement and to tell the bartender that the next time he sends anybody after him, he will be buried next to the man he sent. The man rode off as fast as his horse would go. Randy watched the rider, until he was out of sight. He then retrieved the man's gun belt along with his firearm. He hung it over his saddle horn, and then mounted up for his ride on to camp.

When he arrived in camp, he removed the saddle from his horse and picketed it near some grass. He did likewise with his packhorse. He then placed a pot of water by the horses. After they were settled, he made his meal and, when done, he sat back sipping his coffee. He removed all the coins from his pocket and was amazed with how much he had accumulated in such a short time. He withdrew the bag from the cave and placed all the coins in it. He took out several bills and placed them in his pocket. Once he settled back down, he poured himself another cup of coffee.

After thinking for a time about what had just occurred, he decided he was going back to the settlement in the morning for breakfast, and then on over to the saloon to pay that bartender a little visit. He felt that once he had settled affairs in the settlement, he had better move on to another territory. He was angry, and it made getting a good night of rest most difficult. He did finally fall asleep, but it was an early rising. He saddled his horse, and then packed all of his gear on his horses as well. He checked the cave and the surrounding area to make sure he had missed nothing. When satisfied, he mounted for the ride into the settlement.

Once he arrived, he went on into the eatery. When his belly was full, he felt he needed a couple of items from the mercantile so proceeded on over to it. He made his purchase, and then loaded it in the packsacks. He had paid with silver, and that made the storekeeper happy. He looked over towards the saloon and saw that it was open, so he decided to get right to taking care of business with the bartender. He rode around the far side of the mercantile and tied his horses off in back of the saloon. He had seen a door back there when he visited before.

He tried the door lightly and found it wasn't locked, so he entered slowly. He removed the thong from the hammer of his sidearm and lifted it a little to be sure it was loose in his holster. He spotted the bartender behind the bar cleaning some drinking glasses. Making sure the bartender couldn't see him, he crept to about ten feet in front of the bar where the bartender was standing. The bartender spotted him and slowly worked himself to one end of the bar. The rider he had sent out evidently worked for him, as he was sweeping the floor.

Randy slowly spoke, saying that if he still needed more information about his money, now was the time to be asking. He then ordered the other man over against the bar next to the bartender. Randy noticed the bartender was slowly working his hand down towards the underside of the bar. Randy knew what was there. He didn't expect what happened next. There was a loud blast, and the front of the bar shattered leaving a gaping hole. Randy instinctively drew and placed a hole in the bartender's head.

The sheriff heard the noise and came running into the saloon with his firearm in hand. He asked Randy what all the commotion was about. Randy turned towards the bar swamper and said with a stern voice for him to tell the sheriff the whole story. The man could see that Randy was still holding his sidearm down along his side, out of sight, so the sheriff couldn't see it. The man complied. The sheriff then told Randy to mount his horse and get as far away from this settlement as fast as he could and to not look back. Randy did.

Chapter Eight

Randy mounted up, and then reached over and took hold of his packhorse's lead rope and rode out of the settlement heading east. After he was well out of sight of the prying eyes of the sheriff, he swung north a distance, and then circled around towards the west. He rode several days in that direction and, being he hadn't run into any settlements, he felt it would probably be better if he headed back towards his hideout. He set camp for the night. When morning rolled around, he ate, and then packed camp. When he had mounted up for the long ride ahead of him, he looked around in all directions to make sure it was safe to ride out.

Just as he felt it was safe to begin his ride, he spotted a rider coming towards him from a northwest direction. He waited until the rider was slightly past him, and then he rode out into the open and stopped. He unhooked the safety thong, and then called out to the rider. It startled the rider. Randy yelled that it was a friendly call and there was no need for a firearm. Randy held his arms out to his side to show the rider that his hands were empty.

They both slowly rode towards each other. Once they were within twenty yards or so of each other, they both reigned up. Randy asked the man if there was a settlement anywhere in the direction from which he had come. The rider said that he had just left one that was maybe four or five miles in the direction from which he had come. Randy thanked the rider and whipped his horses towards that settlement. He was really glad to find out that, indeed, there was a settlement in the direction in which he desired to travel.

Randy arrived at the settlement in the mid-morning and immediately sought out the liveryman. His horse was showing signs that something wasn't right with one of its rear hoofs. When he arrived, the liveryman came out to greet him. When Randy told him of the problem his mount was having, the man immediately went to the leg that Randy had pointed to. He lifted the horse's leg and placed it between his legs.

Randy dismounted and walked around to where he could see what was going on. The liveryman said that the horse had evidently stepped on something sharp and cut the tender portion of the hoof. He asked Randy how big a hurry he was in. Randy told the man that it depended on whether the sheriff would run him out of the settlement. The man laughed, and then explained that he could place a full cover plate on as a shoe, and it would protect the horse from injuring its hoof any further. He went on to say that the shoe should be removed after a week or so.

Randy told the man to go ahead and put the protective shoe on, and he would just stick around until the liveryman decided the horse was healed. He went on to tell the man to corral and feed the horses until his mount was ready. The liveryman told Randy that, being he didn't know him, he would have to pay in advance. He said it wasn't because he didn't trust him, it's just that he has had a few run out without paying before, and he couldn't afford to have that happen again. Randy told him that he understood and handed the man one of the paper bills he had. Randy told the liveryman that he could give him the change when he came to get his horses.

Randy then left for the hotel, carrying his saddlebags. He asked for a room that overlooked the street in front of the building and booked it for a week. He had his reason for it. Once in the room, he placed the saddlebags on the table, and then went to the window to see if his room could be accessed from the outside. He noticed that the window had heavy bars attached on the outside of it. He grabbed hold of the bars and gave them a violent jerk to make sure they couldn't come loose. Once he was satisfied that his room was secure, he placed his personal items on the table. He had a great deal of money in his saddlebags.

He turned to leave the room and noticed that there were two heavy-duty deadbolts on the inside of the door. He liked that. He left the room, locking the door securely, and when he arrived at the desk, he asked the clerk why all the security items were in his room. The clerk told him that a gold miner had hit it rich, and when he rented that room, he ordered the protective items to be installed. He went on to say that the miner had paid handsomely for it. Randy told the man that if anybody broke in to rob his room, they would be mighty disappointed, as he was so broke. They both laughed.

Randy then left for the saloon. While he was walking towards the saloon, he pulled the brim of his hat down low over his eyes. He had learned that his eyes would adjust to the darker interior of the saloon much faster— you never knew who might be on the other side of the batwing doors. He stepped in and slid off to one side, which was his usual habit, and then lifted the brim of his hat back up. He spotted the bar and walked over to it and ordered a whisky—the good stuff! He laid down one of the bills, and when he received his change, he stuffed it in his pocket.

While sipping his whisky, he glanced around the place and spotted the poker tables in the far end of the room. Nobody was playing, so he tossed down the remainder of his whisky and left for the eatery. He sat himself where he could see the door and out the window across the street. When the waitress arrived at his table, he ordered coffee and a beef sandwich. When she returned with his food, he asked her where the next settlement was heading west. She said it was just a short distance past her ranch. That puzzled him.

She left for another table, and Randy commenced to devour his meal. When she came back to refill his cup, he asked her why she was working here if she owned a ranch. She was an extremely attractive, dark-haired lady. She said that her husband was a rowdy person and ran into the wrong person over at a settlement east of here. She went on to say that he got into a gunfight with the man and was killed. Randy asked her if she was working here to support the ranch, and she said that was the reason. Randy felt bad for her and left an extremely large tip on the table. Randy repeated the tipping process all week long while waiting for his horse to heal.

He played a few hands of poker, always using a bill and dragging change. One of the players was getting antsy about his using a bill to bet with all the time. Randy explained that he had sold his ranch back East to a wealthy neighbor and had been paid in bills. He also said that there were times that he couldn't use the bills, so he needed the gold and silver to pay with. That seemed to satisfy the man. Randy would purposely lose a hand every so often, but always managed to leave a winner. Each night he deposited the gold and silver in his saddlebag and took out several more of the bills.

After a week and a half, his horse had finally healed up and was feeling pretty spunky. The liveryman removed the steel plate, and then placed the old shoe back on the horse. He had recently had new shoes put on his horse, so there was no need for a new one. Each day he had given his horse a good workout by taking it up steep hillsides in soft dirt. He would never let it run, as he didn't want to damage the hoof any more than it was. His horse seemed to be in pretty good shape for all it had been through.

Randy decided it was time for him to move on and would settle up with everyone in the morning. He would take it easy on his horse for the next few weeks to make sure the hoof was well healed. He would only run the horse if the need was great enough.

When morning rolled around, Randy packed his gear, settled with the desk clerk, and headed to the livery for his horse and the change he had coming. Once that was settled, he headed to the eatery to fill his belly before he began his trek towards the next settlement. While eating his meal, the waitress came over to refill his cup. Randy told her that he was on his way to that settlement she had told him about. He told her that if he ever meandered this way again, he would drop in and see her. She told him that if she wasn't here, to drop in at the ranch. She said he would be welcome at either place. Randy bid her goodbye. As he rose to leave, he told her that he felt embarrassed that he didn't even know her name. She smiled and told him that it was Pat. Randy then told her his name. She said she already knew.

Chapter Nine

It was a little better than a day and a half before Randy came across the waitress's ranch. He felt she must stay in the settlement all week and only ride back to the ranch when she needed a day or so off. It was too far to commute very often. He rode on over to the ranch house and really felt bad for how badly the place had deteriorated from the lack of maintenance. He was in no hurry so set camp in a small grove of trees. He then commenced to make some of the necessary repairs. He didn't want to infringe too much, so he left after the third day.

Randy had made a big dent in the needed repairs. The door to the house wasn't locked, so he found an envelope, placed several of the bills in it. He then wrote a short note saying that he hoped the money would help her until she found whatever her future had in store for her. Randy then left for the settlement that was supposed to be west of the ranch. He was whistling a tune as he rode away from the ranch. It gave him great satisfaction to be able to do something for the lady.

Randy found out quickly that Pat's interpretation of a short distance was quite different than his. It wasn't until mid-morning on the third day that Randy rode into the settlement. He immediately sought out the livery and boarded his horse for the stay. He then found the hotel and booked his room for a week. The saloon was next. He located it and settled in for a few drinks. It was getting on towards evening, and his belly reminded him that he had been neglecting it, so he went to the eatery and satisfied his hunger.

He then returned to the saloon for a few hands of poker. At each place he had played, he had been able to use some of the bills to pay with. While playing poker, he did the same until he began to make a few of the players a little nervous about it. It was the same each day, until he began to feel uncomfortable with the looks he was starting to get from all those with whom he had done business. He decided to explain it away in the same manner he had at the last settlement, by telling them he had sold his ranch back East. It seemed to satisfy everybody, as the stares discontinued. It even settled down the card players. He was glad, as he still wanted to stay a little longer.

The pile of bills he had left over from the stagecoach robbery was dwindling down much faster than he anticipated, and the gold and silver coins were becoming too heavy to continue to carry around. He had to find a solution for them. He finally felt he might be wearing out his welcome so decided to move on in the morning. He had heard about another settlement to the south, so felt that would be his next place to go. All those coins were still bothering him. All of a sudden Randy remembered the cave he had camped by and felt that it might just be the place to stash the coins until he had all the bills taken care of.

When morning rolled around, he packed up and settled all of his bills, again using the bills to pay with. Once he had stocked up on all the supplies he would need, he rode south towards that settlement. It took several days to reach it. He thought he might be getting a little too close to where he had robbed the stagecoach. As he rode through the settlement looking for the livery, he spotted a man who looked familiar. The man hadn't spotted Randy yet, so he rode in between two buildings and stopped.

As he watched the man, he became too nervous about it and decided to head for that cave instead. He felt the cave should be located several days ride east of this settlement, so he remounted his horse and rode around the back of the businesses to avoid being seen by that man. He rode south a couple of miles, and then turned west.

It was several days later when the territory he was riding across began to look familiar. He recognized several outcroppings he had passed when he was looking for a place to camp on his way north and getting away from those who were looking for him.

Randy rode on over to the outcroppings and found where he had camped by that cave. It was located on a hillside just north of the two outcroppings. After looking the area over, he was satisfied that it would be a safe place to stash the money. He set camp up and picketed his horses near some water. He removed all the gear from his mount, and the saddle hit the ground with a thud from all the weight in the saddlebags. He had always removed the saddlebags before he removed the saddle. He couldn't believe how heavy they had become.

He removed the saddlebags and carried them to the fire. He had several sacks that held his supplies, so he emptied one and placed the money in it. He struggled to place the bag far in the back of the small cave, as it was so heavy. He stacked rocks in front of it. He then threw dirt all over the rocks, making it look entirely impossible to find unless, someone had a reason to dig deeper into the cave. He patted himself on the back for his bit of ingenuity, and then settled in for the night.

When morning rolled around, he was quite surprised at how late he had slept. The sun was full up, and it was becoming fairly warm already. He decided that this would be a good place to hide out for a while. On the fourth day, his curiosity got the best of him, and he made the decision to return to his old hideout. He would ride out in the morning at first light. Making sure the cave was obscure, making the money safe from prying eyes, he mounted up for the long trek.

He arrived at a point where he could see the surrounding area around his escape route from the backup place where he kept his packhorse. He glassed the area over thoroughly. Seeing no sign of anybody, he approached the entrance to the hiding place. Some of his old supplies were still there. He had left in such a hurry, that he didn't have time to pack it all. He worked his way over to the escape trail from his hideout. Randy was beginning to shake and wondered if all the curiosity was worth it.

He slowly worked his way down towards the side entrance to his old hideout. When he reached the bottom and came to the tunnel to camp, he removed his sidearm and readied it for action, if needed. He slowly approached the opening, listening for any sounds that might be out of the ordinary and possibly a danger to him. When he reached the end of the tunnel, he slowly parted the brush covering to look around.

He was relieved to find the area deserted. He worked his way to where he could see the flat down below and again was relieved to see no one there either. He had one last task, and that was to check the watering hole to see if that had been compromised. When he had made his way to the spring, he found signs of only a few animals having used the spring. He took a long drink from the pool, and then warily made his way back to the hideout. He looked around and saw a few boot tracks here and there, but no sign that anybody had been observing this camp.

Randy worked his way up towards the upper hideout. When he was about to emerge into the opening, he heard voices. He quickly slid, on his hands and knees, off to the side through the thick underbrush. He came to an animal trail heading in the direction of his tied-up horses. He hoped they hadn't discovered his horses and that they would still be there when he arrived. When he exited the brush, he spotted his mount and packhorse about twenty yards away, so he made a run for it. As soon as he was in the saddle, he whipped the horse into a dead run towards the east.

Chapter Ten

As Randy was riding hard, he heard shouts saying he was getting away. He heard shots ring out and the snap of the bullets as they slammed past his head. He now knew that he had stepped into a trap, and somebody had been watching his hideouts. All of a sudden, he felt a sting between his left arm and side. He had been hit in the meaty part of his ribs on the outside. He reached over and felt the gouge in the side of his ribs. He pulled his hand back and saw that it was covered with his blood. That scared him even more, and he whipped his horses into a harder run.

He felt another bullet hit him in the meaty portion of his right shoulder. He was hit hard. He had to get up into the mountains where he could find a way to escape his pursuers. He felt the slam of another bullet into the upper portion of his left hip. How he was able to stay in the saddle was a mystery to him. He was hurting unbearably. It wasn't but a few seconds later when he felt the slam of another bullet in his right side. The bullet had gone clear through.

Randy finally broke over the ridge and turned north, looking for a place in which to either hide or escape. He spotted a solid rock stretch, and rode up onto it. He traveled east on it until he could see that it was about to end. He circled around towards the west and found a large patch of brush. He spurred his horses towards it and when they reached it, the horses made a jump over and into it with a mighty lunge. Somehow the horses kept on running through it, and on out the other side.

Randy turned his horses north for a ways, and then west on down off the hill. When he reached the bottom and out onto the flat, he kept his horses on a dead run in a northwest direction. He was slowly losing his strength. He had been badly shot up, and it was an absolute miracle that he was still able stay in the saddle. He came to a knoll and rode it up from the backside. When he was about to top out, he pulled in behind some brush. He looked over the area from the direction he had come and saw no one. That was a relief.

Now the pain from the wounds was setting in. It was horrendous. The blood was everywhere he looked on his body. He felt faint but knew he couldn't allow that to happen until he found help. He turned and rode on towards the only help he felt he could trust.

Pat's ranch was several days' ride northwest, and he had already been in the saddle for a day and a half without stopping. He only hoped his horses could hold up until he reached the ranch. He caught himself about to fall off his horse numerous times as he rode. There were times he woke up still sitting in the saddle, holding on to the saddle horn.

He wondered what was keeping him in the saddle. He had been delirious from time to time. He had ridden through two nights and knew that something more powerful than anything earthly could be holding him upright in the saddle. The blood had quit oozing from his body two nights ago. He had been extremely fortunate that none of the bullets had hit any bones or vital organs. He knew his time was running out if he didn't find help soon. He felt he should reach Pat's ranch sometime in the late afternoon, if he could just stay in the saddle.

After a time, he lifted his head to look around at his surroundings and spotted a ranch house off in the far distance. He headed straight for it. He didn't care whose ranch it was. He just knew he needed help. *Now!* It seemed like an eternity had gone by before he reached the house. He rode over to where the porch was and slid his mount sideways up against it. He tried to yell out for help, but nothing came forth from his mouth. He began to slide off the horse towards the porch, and then hit it with a thud. His left foot was still hung up in the stirrup. Everything went black.

When he regained consciousness, he was totally delirious. He had no idea where he was or how he had got there. All he knew was that he hurt like hell everywhere on his body—or certainly it seemed like everywhere. He knew he was in a soft bed under warm blankets. He had bandages all over his body and was in a man's long nightgown. He was sweating profusely. He heard himself moaning; no wonder, as he hurt so badly. He had a severe headache. He touched his head and felt a very large bump on the left front of his forehead.

He could hear footsteps approaching his bed. He couldn't focus his eyes on whomever it was. He then felt a cold rag being placed across his forehead, covering the large bump. *It felt good.* He tried focusing his eyes, but to no avail. He then felt a soft hand caressing his face and hair. He tried to speak, but a woman's voice told him to lie still. Her voice sounded so soothing. The lady asked him if he thought he could eat some soup. He was just barely able to nod his head up and down. She left his side and returned with a bowl of warm soup. It smelled really good. She began spooning the soup through his lips, slowly. It tasted good. It took quite a while, but in the end she accomplished getting the entire bowl of soup in him. He went out like a light again.

When he regained consciousness, he was able to focus his eyes enough to see foggy surroundings. He could see it was daylight. He could hear noises from the outside of his room. They sounded like they were coming from the kitchen. The sound was of pots and pans being bumped against each other. After some time had passed, he could hear the now-familiar sound of footsteps coming towards the room again. When the door opened, what looked like an angel from heaven came gliding through. *It was Pat!*

When she reached his bedside, she reached down and flipped the blankets back. She said it looked like they had a little cleaning up to do. Randy was embarrassed. She didn't hesitate. She tucked all the sheets up tight against his body. She then tucked a clean one up against that one. She then rolled him over onto the fresh one and lifted out the old one. She spread the new sheet out, and then rolled him over onto the clean sheet. She left the room carrying the old sheet and returned carrying a pot of water and some clothes.

She began to wash his body all over. She didn't stop until she had cleaned his entire body, even his private area. His face was as red as a beet. She then left, carrying the pot of water and dirty clothes. It was quite a while before she returned. She asked him if he was able to sit up a little and eat some stew. He nodded his head yes. She went around to the end of the bed and helped him scoot up onto a couple of pillows. He was able to spoon the stew himself, so she just sat there holding the bowl. It was delicious. She asked him if he wanted some coffee and he told her that he did.

She scooted on out of the room, taking the bowl with her. When she returned, she was carrying a tray with a pot of coffee on it along with two cups. She poured both cups full, and then picked one up to let him sip on it. He told her that he thought he could hold the cup himself. He was shaky but was able to drink it without help. She poured him another and refilled her cup as well. They sipped their coffee together. When the coffee was gone, she took the tray with the cups and pot with her. When she returned, she pulled a chair over to the side of the bed and merely sat there and looked at him.

Finally he asked her how long he had been here. She told him that this was the second week. That took him back a little. She went on to say that she didn't think he was going to live but somehow, after the third or fourth day, things began to turn around. She went on to say that this wasn't quite how she wanted him to come and visit. He stuttered for a moment, and then said he would have to tell her the whole story. She reached over and placed her fingers over his lips and said that he had already told her. That puzzled him. She said that he had told her everything when he was delirious.

They sat there looking at each other for a time.

Then she said that it was all in the past. Not to worry. Nobody in the area knew of his history and, as far as she was concerned, nobody would ever know in the future either. He told her that he didn't even know how he got here. She said she had found him lying on her porch with one foot caught in the stirrup of his saddle. She said he must have landed on her porch and hit his head on something on the way down. She also said that she hoped the bump on his head might have knocked some sense into him.

They both chuckled.

Chapter Eleven

It was another two weeks before Randy had enough strength to get out of bed on his own, but he still needed help getting dressed. He began taking his meals with Pat at the table. All of a sudden he remembered his horses and asked Pat about them. She told him that it took some time, but the horses seemed to be getting better day by day. She then asked him what the heck he had ridden those horses through, as they were all cut up across the bottom of their bellies and on the sides of their legs. Randy told her that he didn't know; he couldn't remember anything after being shot up. He told her that if she needed those answers, she would have to ask the horses.

His healing went slow because of the severity of his the wounds. He had been hit hard four times. Why he survived was a miracle that couldn't be explained. Pat said she hadn't treated a bullet wound before, and, from what he had told her while he was delirious, she decided not to take him to a doctor or bring one out to her ranch. That was out of the question. The doctor would have told the sheriff.

She went on to say that, being as all the bullets had gone clear through instead of lodging inside his body, she felt that treating the wounds like any other open wound would be the way to go. It seemed like it was working, as the wounds were slowly closing up. It was going to take a long, long time before he was completely healed, as so much of the muscle around the path of each bullet had been severely damaged. She had done a great job of keeping the wounds clean and the bandages changed daily. She would continue treating him until he felt he could make it on his own.

After several days more had passed and they were sitting at the table sipping coffee after a great breakfast, she decided to ask him questions about his plans for the future. He told her that he really hadn't given it much thought. He also told her that when he started out on this journey, away from the home he had never been away from before, he sure as heck hadn't planned it to go the way it had. He went on to say that he hated what he was becoming, but it seemed that each incident he encountered dragged him deeper and deeper into this life.

After sitting silently for a time, she rose and retrieved the pot of coffee and refilled their cups. She returned the pot to the stove. When she returned to the table and sat down once more, she looked at him intently for a moment. She broke the silence by telling him that when she returned to the ranch after he had left the settlement, she was quite shocked and very thankful for all the repairs that had been done around there. She said she was even more shocked and thankful for the envelope she found on the table. He told her that he didn't have anything better to do at the time and it just seemed like the right thing to do.

She sat there with tears forming in her eyes. He said that if she didn't mind, he would like to hang around after he healed up to complete the rest of the needed repairs. She told him that she couldn't afford to pay him. She said that she wouldn't mind feeding and boarding him while he was here and that he was welcome to stay in the house if he desired. He winked at her and told her that she had better watch out, as he was a mighty dangerous man. They laughed.

They finished their coffee, and she suggested that they sit out on the front porch for a while. He said he felt that would be a great change from going to the table and back to bed repeatedly. They rose and walked out to the porch and sat next to each other in rocking chairs. He told her that it had been a mighty long time since he had rocked in one of these chairs. She said that the last time the chair was used was when her husband was alive. Randy started to get up and apologize for sitting in that rocker. She sternly stated for him to sit back down. He did.

It was pretty early yet and the sun was still low in the morning sky. They sat there rocking back and forth and talking about all the needed repairs. Randy made the mistake of telling her that he could get started on the repairs in the morning. She jumped up and said that he certainly was not going to do any work for the next several weeks. Randy started to say something more but she just stated that it was the end of that kind of silly talk. She stomped off into the house. He kind of got the idea that she meant what she said.

Randy just sat there rocking back and forth for another two and a half hours before Pat came back out. She found him with his head slumped forward. As she approached him to see if he was all right, she could hear him snoring very lightly. She had brought with her a piece of pie and another pot of coffee. She placed them on the table between them and went back to the kitchen for their cups. When she returned, Randy was sitting there looking down at the pie. She told him good morning and sat down. His head popped upright and he stuttered his reply of good morning.

She poured the coffee and set the pot back down. He asked her if the pie was for eating or looking at. She put a scowl on her face and started to reach for his plate, so he reached out and grabbed it before she could pick it up. He knew what that look meant. They laughed. It felt good for the two of them to be able to laugh together. They had been too serious for quite some time now. Together they enjoyed the fresh apple pie. After it was devoured, they sat and enjoyed the coffee. The scenery around the ranch was magnificent. He felt at peace.

Randy asked her if she felt it would be all right if they walked over to the corral so he could see his horses. She reluctantly agreed to do so. When they arrived, the horses spotted them and ran over to Randy. The horses began rubbing their noses up and down on Randy's cheeks. Tears formed in Randy's eyes. Pat watched with tears forming in her own eyes as well. She was glad that she had agreed to let him stay. She slipped off further into the barn and returned carrying a bench. She placed it close to the back of Randy's legs so he could sit down. She then sat down beside him. Both of them took turns scratching the horses here and there. The horses were eating it up.

After a half hour had gone by, they returned to the house and again sat in the rocking chairs. It became lunch time, and Pat made a couple of beef and cheese sandwiches. It was good. Randy started showing signs of wearing out, so she helped him back to his bed. Once there and lying down, he fell asleep immediately. She reached over and gently tucked him in. She went about her own business. She wondered where all this would lead. Her only money came from working at the eatery. She was now going to have to head back to the settlement again.

She had a large loan she had taken on. She did that so she could hold on to the ranch, and now she was struggling to make the payments. She had to keep up with those payments or she would lose the ranch. She made the decision to leave first thing in the early morning hours. She packed a few items and set them by the door. She then put on a pot of stew for dinner. Once she had that all in place, she went to the door, picked up the bag, and headed on out to the barn. She readied everything for her ride to the settlement in the morning.

Randy woke up just before dark. He still had his clothes on, so went into the living room. Pat was sitting there thumbing through some magazines that had been lying around. She looked up at Randy and smiled. She asked him if he was hungry, and he said that he was. She told him there was a pot of stew on and ready. They wasted no time getting to it. She said nothing about her plans. When their meal was consumed, they retired to the front porch and sipped coffee while rocking away. It turned late, so they turned in for the night.

Chapter Twelve

When Randy awoke, he got up and went into the kitchen and sat down. Pat was not anywhere that he could see or hear. He called out for her and heard no answer. The coffee was hot on the stove. He poured himself a cup, and then slipped out onto the porch and sat down on the rocking chair. While sipping on his coffee, he spotted movement coming from the direction of the barn. He watched intently for a moment, and then saw Pat riding out in her buggy, drawn by a nice looking horse. She pulled along the side of the porch and said good morning to Randy. He asked her where she was going, and she explained how she needed to go back to work.

Randy looked intently at her for a moment. He asked her to step down and join him for coffee. He said that he had something he wanted to tell her. She stepped down, went into the house and retrieved the pot of coffee along with another cup, and then returned to the porch. She sat down in her rocking chair, and then reached over and refilled Randy's cup. She then filled her own. They sat there staring at each other for a moment. She finally broke the silence and asked him if he was planning on pulling out. He immediately told her that it wasn't anything like that.

She said that she had to go back to work as she needed to earn money to pay on her ranch dept. He stopped her, and then said he had a better solution to that, if she would go along with it. She blurted out that she wasn't going to sell the ranch. He said that was the furthest thing from his mind. She said for him to spit it out. He told her that he had money and could help her out with all her problems. She told him that she saw the money he had and it wouldn't solve things for very long. He just laughed and said he had more than that.

He then looked at her seriously and said he had something to tell her that she would not like, but the facts were the facts. She told him not to beat around the bush and get it out, as she needed to get on the trail. He began explaining that he had enough money to pay off her debt and much, much more. She asked him where he had gotten it. He began by telling her that he had gone astray when he had left his home in Gila Bend and turned to gambling and more serious things after a time.

She looked hard at him and asked him just how serious were those other things. He said that he started robbing people to get money to gamble with. She didn't say anything. He went on to say that, after a time he got greedy and robbed a stage coach. Her face didn't change. He went on to say that, during the robbery, a man forced him to shoot him when he started to yell out his name. Randy said, had the man done that, everybody would have known it was him who had robbed the coach. He said that the man spoke just enough of his name that, when the coach got back to the settlement and the word of the dying man had spread, one person put the pieces together and identified the robber as Randy.

She still sat there without changing the expression on her face. He went on to tell her that he made it back to his hideout and stashed the money. He told her that when he had tallied up his take, he was shocked to find it to be an extremely tidy sum. He said that he knew he had to get the jewelry sold and the money placed in a safe place. He went on to tell her that once he had done that, he stashed all the money in a small cave. As far as he knew, the money was still there.

She didn't say a thing. She just sat there listening to what he had to say. He went on to tell her that he made the decision to ride on down to his old hideout to see if it had been compromised. He said that once he was there, he found that all seemed to be in place and maybe it would be a safe place to return to from time to time. He said that while he was crawling up through his escape trail, he heard voices just outside of the tunnel. He told her that he crawled on his hands and knees off to the side and found a tunnel that the animals had been using and headed to where his horses were.

He told her that when he mounted up on his horse and took up the lead rope for the packhorse, one of the men spotted him and the chase began. That is when the shooting started. He went on to say that she knew the rest of the story, and he had no idea what happened between the time the shooting started and he woke up in the bed. She just stared at him for a time, and then asked him if his wild days were over or was he going back to robbing and killing. Again she sat there staring at him.

Randy finally spoke. He said that she had seen what shape he was in when she found him. He said that he had no plan to get into the types of messes he had gotten himself into after he left his home in Gila Bend. He said that all he wanted was a little more excitement in his life than what he had there. After a short moment of silence, she told him that she already knew most of the story, as he spoke of it while he was so delirious. She asked him what his plans were . . . to move on or what.

He told her that she now knew the rest of the story, and he would only leave if she wanted him to. He told her that he didn't want her to get into any trouble because of his past. He said that if she was willing, they could leave immediately and retrieve the money from that cave and get things in order with her ranch. She looked at him for what seemed like forever, and then told him that she wasn't going to feed him to the dogs and would like it if he stayed on as a ranch hand.

Randy slumped back with a relaxed and relieved look. She went on to tell him that she wasn't going to hold his past against him. She said that only the future knows what the past will bring with it. Randy thanked her with tears in his eyes. She told him that happier days would be in his future, as long as he was done with his past life. He assured her that his past was over. He said that he longed for a peaceful life, the likes of which he had not known for a long, long time. He said that all he wanted was to be happy and settle down again. She stood up and asked him if he was hungry. He nodded his head yes.

They went into the kitchen, and while Randy sat there with tears in his eyes, she fixed his meal. She began placing some items in a basket. When the basket was filled with all that it could hold, she placed it by the door. As she turned towards her bedroom, she stopped and asked Randy how far it was to where he had the money stashed. He told her that it would be a long day's ride. She asked him if he thought the buggy would make it there. He told her that he didn't think that would be a wise choice. He then smiled and asked her if that meant she would take him up on his offer. She smiled and said yes.

Tears rolled down the cheeks of both of them. She asked him if he felt he could last the ride in a saddle. Randy got up and told her that they should saddle up his mount and see if he could climb onto it. They went out to the corral to saddle up his horse. Once he had the reigns on the horse, he threw a blanket over its back, and then reached over and lifted the saddle. It hurt like hell, and he dropped it back down on the rail. Pat saw that and said she was convinced that he couldn't handle it yet and that the buggy was their only choice.

They walked back towards the house and, while Randy stood by the wagon, Pat went in and retrieved the basket. She placed it in the wagon, and then went back in and came back out with an armload of bedding and placed that in the buggy as well. She climbed up on the buggy, took up the reins of the horse, and told Randy to get aboard. He gingerly complied. She whipped the horse into action. As they pulled out of the yard, she told Randy to start giving directions or they would be as lost as anybody had ever been. They both laughed.

Chapter Thirteen

It was a slow ride, as every time the wagon hit a bump Randy winced with pain. They stopped for an hour or so every once in a while to give Randy a chance to recover. They both knew it was going to be a very long ride. They would never make it there in one day. They had to weave in and around every rock, bush, and any other obstacle in their path, of which there was an abundance. It had been a long day as the sun began its decent on the horizon. They found a small patch of greenery off in the distance and decided to try and make it there before dark beset them.

When they reached the patch, they found a small spring in the middle of the greenery. It was a perfect place to make camp for the night. Darkness was coming upon them, so they hustled to make a fire. Pat spread her bedroll out in the wagon. Randy was heating up the leftover stew Pat had brought along. He had a pot of coffee brewing, and by the time the stew was hot, the coffee was in a hard boil. Pat came over by his side and sat down. They enjoyed their meal and savored the coffee to the last drop before they were ready to turn in.

Randy went to retrieve his bedroll when he discovered that they had forgotten to put it in the buggy. Pat had already climbed up into the buggy and was tucked in for the night. Randy asked her if she could spare one of her blankets. She told him to crawl under the blankets with her, but to make danged sure he stayed on his side. They laughed hard for quite some time and chuckled every so often, until each slipped off into a deep sleep. It had been a rough, hard day and had taken its toll on Randy.

When Randy woke, up the sun was just beginning to rise above the horizon. Randy felt Pat cuddled up against his back. He didn't move for fear of waking her up. She had been through a living hell with him the past few weeks. He wanted her to get all the sleep she could to help her recover as well. It was another hour before Pat began to stir. When she realized that she was cuddled up to Randy's back, she slowly moved away and rolled over onto her back. Randy didn't move and pretended he was still asleep. He didn't want to embarrass Pat.

After a few minutes had passed, Randy pretended he was just waking up. He yawned and pulled the covers tighter against his neck, and then just lay there. After a few more minutes had passed, Pat gently slid out of the blankets, quietly climbed down out of the wagon, and commenced to stoke the fire back up. She added some small twigs to the coals, and the fire immediately roared to life. She added some more wood to the fire, and then fixed a pot of coffee. She had brought some slices of roast beef and placed them in the skillet along with some eggs. She placed several biscuits on top of the roast beef.

When the coffee began to boil, she walked over to the wagon and nudged Randy to wake him up. He rolled over and looked up at Pat and said good morning to her. She asked him if he was going to sleep his whole life away. They chuckled. She then told him that their breakfast was ready. He crawled out from under the blankets and stepped down out of the buggy. They both sat down by the fire and enjoyed their breakfast. The coffee was especially good.

When the last of the coffee was consumed, they packed up everything and hitched the horse back up to the buggy. Randy couldn't stand it anymore and said that it sure had been warm under those blankets, especially his back, and began to climb aboard. She grabbed him by his shirt and stopped him and called him a big phony. She said he knew all along that she had accidently rolled against his back. He started laughing hard. He then said that she accidently rolled up good and snuggly against his back. He really laughed hard again. It was hurting his side. She told him that maybe that would teach him to be such a big phony. They laughed hard together.

They climbed up in the buggy, and then Pat whipped the horse into action. They slowly picked their way towards their destination and finally reached the cave just after high noon. Randy wasted no time showing Pat where the money was hidden and explained that if she scraped the dirt away and removed the rocks, she would find the bag containing the money behind it all.

Pat excitely began removing the dirt and rocks. She saw the bag, took hold of the top, and dragged it out of the cave. It was really heavy. She wasted no time opening the bag. When she saw all the gold and silver, she began to sob. When she finally calmed down, she told Randy that she really hadn't believed him when he said there was so much hidden money. She lifted the bag with a struggle and placed it in the buggy under the blankets. She then placed the basket of food up against it. They both climbed up into the wagon and began their trek back towards the ranch.

They reached the ranch late on the second day after they had retrieved the money. It was a welcome relief. They took the bag of money into the house. Pat walked over to a chair and moved it off of a small rug. Under the rug was a two-foot-by-two-foot door. She lifted up the door and placed the money down into a concrete vault. She then placed the door back in its place, and then spread the rug over it and placed the chair back on top of it. She stood back and smiled at Randy. He stood there shaking his head.

Pat went into the kitchen and built a fire in the cook stove. She then placed a pot of coffee on. She went back out to the wagon and retrieved the blankets and basket. She placed the basket on the table and headed to her bedroom to place the blankets back on her bed. Randy called out and asked her if they would have the same sleeping arrangement for tonight. He laughed. She told him to forget that notion.

When Pat had finished with the bedding, she headed back to the kitchen to make dinner. Randy had beaten her to it. He had a cup of coffee on the table across from where he sat. He had place-settings out on the table ready for their meal. She sat down and enjoyed the coffee. When Randy had their meal ready, he took Pat's plate and dished hers up first, and then did likewise with his. It was a delicious meal. When the dishes were cleaned, they both turned in immediately, as they were exhausted.

Chapter Fourteen

When morning rolled around and they had consumed their breakfast, they sat out on the porch in the rocking chairs enjoying their coffee. They both had a peaceful look about themselves. Randy suggested that they settle up with the banker. She agreed. He asked her how much she had left on the loan. She got up and went inside the house and, after a moment or two, returned with the contract and most recent receipt showing the payment and balance remaining. She was a week overdue on her payment. Randy told her to get out enough gold and silver to pay off the loan and take a little extra in case they charged her a late fee.

They made the decision to leave immediately for the settlement. Pat was like a happy child. She was so excited about being in a position where no one could ever take her ranch away from her. Things had really been hard on her since she had lost her husband. Trying to live on the measly sum she collected as a waitress and paying down the loan had really put her through trying times. Randy went out and hitched the horse up to the buggy. He then pulled the buggy up to the front of the house.

Pat had the money in a small bag when she stepped up into the buggy. Randy took the bag from her and tucked it up under the seat in a small compartment that couldn't be seen unless you put your head down inside the foot-well and looked up. It was where tools were kept in case they were needed for making repairs. To access the tool box, you had to lift the seat. He wasn't going to take any chances. He whipped the horse into motion.

It was quite late when they reached the settlement. They had to wake the hotel clerk up so they each could get a room. Once Randy had the money safely in his room, he rode the buggy over to the livery, unhitched the horse, and turned it loose in the corral. He would make things right with the livery owner in the morning. He returned to the hotel and went to Pat's door to be sure she was all right. He told her to be sure and lock her door, and then he said good night. He returned to his room and, after making sure his room was secure, he turned in for the night.

Morning rolled around and, with it, excitement to be taking care of the loan at the bank. It didn't take them long to get dressed, packed, and meet down at the desk to pay for the rooms. They left the hotel and headed over to the livery to retrieve the horse and buggy and make things square with the liveryman. Once that was taken care of, they rode the buggy on over to the eatery. The breakfast seemed to taste extra good this morning, which probably was from their feelings of excitement. Once breakfast was consumed, they made their way over to the bank.

Their timing was good, as the banker had just arrived and was opening the door. They walked in with him and sat waiting for the banker to get all of his usual opening chores completed. Once he had all in order, he walked to his desk and sat down. He stared at the two of them, and then broke the silence and asked them what he could do for them. He had kind of a sneer on his face. They rose and walked over, and Pat sat down in front of the banker's desk.

Once she was settled, with Randy standing by her side, she pulled out her bank note and reached over and took the money and placed it on the desk. She then told the banker she wanted to pay off her outstanding loan on the ranch. The banker rose up and went over to his file cabinet and took out her file. He stood there looking at the open file for a moment, and then returned to sit down at his desk.

He looked up at her and told her that it appeared she was delinquent on the loan, and the ranch had been put in foreclosure. She protested that it was only a week late. He just sat there with that smug look on his face and said that he was sorry but there was no alternative. Randy reached down and undid the thong on the hammer of his sidearm. The banker's eyes opened wide when he saw that. Randy looked the banker in the eyes and, with a cold calculated look, told him he might want to reconsider that decision.

The banker then stammered and said that maybe he had been a little premature with that decision. He went on to say that he always tried to be fair and considerate in his dealings with his clients. He looked down at the file and said that he would have to charge her a late fee. Randy replaced the thong and told the banker to get it done. The banker then gave her the final figure that would fully and completely satisfy the loan.

Pat began counting out the money, and when she had the correct amount stacked in front of her, she reached out and slid it all within the banker's reach. Randy looked at the banker with that same look and told him to write the lady a receipt that stated the loan was now satisfied with full and complete payment of the dept. When the banker had the note prepared, Randy told him to sign the receipt. The banker complied with a sour look on his face. He then slid it over to Pat.

Randy reached down and took the receipt from Pat and looked it over. Once satisfied that all was in order, Randy looked the banker in the eyes again and told him that it had been nice doing business with such a reputable banker. Pat stood up, and the two of them left the bank. Once outside, they immediately climbed up into the buggy, and Pat whipped the horse into a gallop. It would be a joyful ride home to her free and clear ranch. Pat looked up at Randy and smiled. She told him thanks. Randy just winked at her with a big smile on his face.

It was well into dark when they arrived at the ranch. Randy wasted no time taking care of the horse and buggy. When he made his way into the house, he was met with the aroma of freshly brewed coffee and Pat at the stove finishing preparing their meal. She reached over and took up the pot of coffee and poured the steaming brew into the two cups on the table. She replaced the pot on the stove and dished up two plates of fried potatoes, steak, and beans. She placed the two plates on the table, and then sat across from Randy with a big smile on her face.

She told Randy that she owed him a big debt for what he had just done for her. He told her that he still owed her a much bigger debt for having saved his life. She told him that he would have a full time job here at the ranch for as long as he wanted to stay. She went on to tell him that she didn't know how she could do any more. Randy looked at her with a smile and told her that maybe she could place the blankets back out in the back of the buggy and they could sleep out there for the night. She told him to get that thought out of his mind, finish his meal, and get to his own bed. They laughed. It had been a great day.

Chapter Fifteen

When morning rolled around, Pat and Randy got up early and prepared themselves for the task of rebuilding the much-neglected ranch. Once breakfast was behind them, they retired to the rocking chairs out on the porch, each with a fresh cup of coffee. In their conversation, the subject of restocking the ranch with livestock came up. Pat told Randy about a large ranch located quite a distance to the north of them where her husband used to purchase cattle. She said he always bought young stock and raised them to butcher for the locals in the nearby settlements.

Randy thought about that for some time. He told Pat that she should consider heading in a different direction from the type of a ranch hers had been. She asked him what his thoughts were on it. He told her that he felt she should buy breeding stock and become self-sufficient. She liked the idea. She told him that was why she hired him. She told him to get the job done. They laughed. Randy said that he would have to make quite a few repairs around the ranch before they could head out on an adventure such as that.

Just as they were about to finish their coffee, the thought of the rancher who had lost his family came to mind. Randy told Pat it might be possible that some of his livestock could still be roaming around out on the hillsides surrounding the ranch. He said that if the Indians hadn't got them all, there might just be enough left to get them started with a herd. Pat smiled and told Randy to get the horses saddled and ready to ride.

Randy smiled and asked Pat if she could ride a horse. She tossed what coffee she had left in her cup at him and said that she probably could ride and rope better then him. She stood up, took Randy's cup along with hers, and took the pot and cups back into the kitchen. Randy saddled the horses, which caused him much pain, and led them to the front of the house. Pat came out with two bags of food along with a bag containing the coffee pot, cups, and coffee grounds. She handed them to Randy, and then headed back into the house but stopped just short of the door. Randy could see the excitement building in Pat. She turned and looked at Randy for a moment, and then told him to remove his shirt, as she wanted to check his wounds to make sure he had not torn them open when he saddled the horses. All seemed to be all right. She then proceeded back into the house.

When Pat returned, she was carrying two bedrolls. Randy smiled at her and asked her why there were two. She threw them at him. They both laughed. He tied them off on the back of the saddles. He then slung the bags over the front of the saddle. Pat went back into the house and, when she returned, she was carrying her rifle along with some extra ammunition. She had on a pair of denim britches, denim jacket, and riding boots. The kicker was that she had a firearm strapped on her side as well. When Randy saw that, he almost went into shock. He saw her in a whole new light. He hadn't, in his wildest dreams, ever envision her decked out like that. It excited him.

She walked around to the other side of her horse and mounted up like an old pro. She scowled down at him and asked him if he was just going to stand there gawking or ride. Randy merely shook his head and mounted up, wincing as he did so. He told her he liked what he saw. She told him that was all he was going to do—only *see*. They laughed hard and whipped their horses into action. They had traveled for a mile or so when Pat reigned up.

She asked Randy just what kind of an incompetent hand she had hired.

He sat there staring at her, puzzled, and wondered what the hell she meant by that. She then asked him where their ropes were. He laughed and told her he thought they should keep them safe, so he had hung them up on the wall of the barn. They both laughed and returned to the ranch. It wasn't long before they had those ropes, along with extra ropes, tied off along the front side of the saddle, and then they were once again on their way. Randy was really enjoying the ride. They were laughing and joking back and forth the whole way.

It was late when they arrived at the burned-out ranch. They didn't want to stay within sight of the rancher and his family's graves, so they rode partially up through a ravine, and then set their camp. Pat began to fix their meal while Randy gathered firewood. They had talked of staying for two, maybe three days. While sitting by their fire eating their meal, they were pleasantly surprised when four cows came walking within their sight. They knew there might be more if those had survived. That was a real uplift.

They hadn't had time yet to erect a temporary corral. Randy spotted a small copse of trees and walked over to them. As he looked around, he spotted a dozen or more trees that could be used together to rope off an area to hold the cows. He went back and saddled his horse, and then took Pat's rope and headed back to that grove of trees. It turned out great, as the way the trees were laid out there would be a place to funnel the cattle through into the corral. Pat rode her horse into the grove and dismounted. She tied her horse off to a tree, and then went to work with Randy to tie the ropes off in the shape of a small corral.

It was now time to see if their little scheme would work. They both mounted up and rode up and over above where they had seen the cows. The cows were still there and had been joined by five more. Randy told Pat that he didn't know if their little corral could hold all of them. Randy circled around to the far side of the herd, and then gently began herding them towards the corral. Pat was a real trooper and evidently had some herding experience. She kept the lead cow headed straight towards the corral.

It wasn't long before they had all of the cows in the overloaded corral. Randy tied a rope across the entry. The two of them stood there looking at what they had in their grips.

They beamed from ear to ear. This had been a real find. All the cows had been branded with the deceased rancher's brand. That was good. There could be no doubt where the cattle had come from, and everybody for miles around had heard of the tragedy that had befallen the rancher and his family. Randy and Pat headed back to their camp.

While sitting by the fire and sipping the remainder of the pot of coffee, they discussed what their next move should be. Randy told Pat that he felt they should just leave camp set up in the morning and make a drive with the cows they already had and get them into Pat's holding pen back at the ranch. This was a magnificent start. They turned in and began what was a most restless night's sleep. It would be quite an exciting morning for them.

Chapter Sixteen

Morning came just as the sun began to peek over the hillside. They made pancakes and bacon for breakfast, as it made for a quick meal. The coffee was a good top-off for the morning meal. When they had their bellies full, they wasted no time getting their horses saddled for the drive. Pat packed leftover pancakes and bacon so they would have something to eat along the way. She placed the coffee pot and some grounds in a bag, and then slung it over the saddle horn. When they were ready, they rode on over to the corral and were pleased that the ropes had done their job.

They slowly removed the ropes and coiled them up then tied them off on the saddles. They mounted up and again slowly rounded the cattle up and began the drive towards Pat's ranch. It was mind boggling how smooth the drive was going. If it kept going this smoothly, they would reach the ranch well into the darkness that night. Only twice did a cow bolt from them, but was quickly recovered. They reached the corral somewhere around ten that night. It had been a blessing to have good moonlight to help them see. They herded the cows into the corral and replaced the gate rails to keep them in.

Randy and Pat both took care of the horses and made sure there was plenty of water in the trough. When done, they went over to the rail and stood looking over their accomplishment. Randy told Pat that it was a mighty good start for her herd. She quickly told Randy that it was *their* herd. She said that if it wasn't for him, they wouldn't have these cows. She said that she would have had to hire someone to bring down a few head from the ranch up north. She went on to say that then she would probably be back in debt.

Randy told Pat that he felt there were more cattle up in that draw. They made plans to make another run for them in the morning. Once they were satisfied that all was well with the cattle, they headed to the house and turned in for a well-deserved night's sleep. It had been a long gruesome trail ride. Herding cattle in the semi-dark is something that not many ranchers would even think of doing. Pat and Randy were successful. It was due to such a small herd. In the morning, they would see just how successful they might be again.

It was an early morning rising, as they wanted to make as early a start as possible. They had much work to be done before they could leave. Once they had completed all the chores, they immediately left for what they had hoped would be a good trip with much success. They arrived at their camp after dark. There was still some moonlight, but it was getting fainter. No time was wasted putting their meal together. They turned in early, as they had another tiring day ahead of them. The hope for another successful find made for a pretty restless night.

When Randy woke, up he heard the crackling of a fire and smelled the aroma of bacon wafting through the air. He rolled over only to see Pat kneeling by the fire making breakfast. Standing nearby were both of their horses all saddled up and ready to go. He sat up and shook his head in amazement. What a woman! He told her good morning. Pat glanced over at him and replied with the same. Randy crawled out of his bedroll and walked over to the fire's edge. Pat handed him a cup of coffee and soon after a plate with bacon, potatoes, and eggs. She dished her plate up, and then sat down across the fire from Randy.

Randy began to apologize for sleeping so late, but Pat stopped him. She told him that he needed all the sleep he could get to drive their herd to the ranch. Randy was puzzled about what she was referring to. She sat there smiling and finished her meal without saying anything more. Once they were done with the meal, she pointed toward the hill and said that they had better get started, as it would be another long, hard day. Randy turned to look where she was pointing, and was really shocked to see eleven more cows all together on the hillside.

Randy looked back at Pat and saw a big grin on her face. Randy began a big grin as well. It couldn't have been any easier than this. Randy told Pat that he was going to take a quick ride up into the draw to see if there were any more. He mounted up and rode off as Pat put things in order in camp. She felt there might be one more trip back here, so didn't bother to pack. She mounted up and rode off in the direction Randy had gone. After she had covered a short distance, she saw Randy herding another one towards her. He had a wide grin on his face.

When they met up, he asked her if she had gotten a good look at the one he was bringing in. She turned and was ecstatic to see that it was a bull. Randy told her that the bull was probably the reason all the cows were together and heading down out of the draw. He told her that he had ridden on farther and, seeing no more cows, had begun the drive to get the bull back to the others. When they reached the others, they corralled the bull, and then rode over to the fire and poured themselves another cup of coffee. Once that was consumed, Randy told Pat he didn't think there were any others. He felt they should pack camp and head for her ranch.

Once they had everything packed, they immediately began to herd the animals down out of the draw. They had cleared the draw and were out into the open when they turned the herd and began heading them straight towards Pat's ranch. Randy and Pat were a couple of extremely happy people. The drive was much harder than the one before, as the bull didn't want to cooperate.

The day turned dark and the moon didn't give them as much light as they wanted. They contemplated about settling down for the night. After discussing it a while, they decided to take their chances and head on towards the ranch.

It was after midnight when they arrived at the ranch and herded the animals into the corral with the others. The bull had really slowed them down. He had become quite cantankerous. They herded the bull off to a separate, smaller pen. After taking care of their horses and making sure all the animals had plenty of water, they wasted no time heading to the house and turning in for the night. It had been a grueling two days.

Morning came quite late for both Pat and Randy. Neither was in a hurry to start doing anything. Randy built a fire in the stove and placed a fresh pot of coffee on the hot stove. He dug out all that would be needed for breakfast. Pat walked into the kitchen just as Randy had their meal ready. He told her good morning, and then pointed towards a chair and said for her to sit while he dished up their breakfast. They sat in silence throughout the entire meal. You could see they were still worn out from all they had accomplished in the past four days.

Randy finally broke the silence. He said that it was an absolute miracle that a week ago she was going to lose the ranch, and now the ranch was free and clear of all debt and fully stocked with a herd of twenty cows plus one mighty fine bull. Pat broke down and began sobbing. Randy got up and took Pat up in his arms and held her tight. It seemed like forever before she finally stopped sobbing. She backed out of his arms and, with tears still running down her cheeks, told him that the blankets were still going to stay where they were. She tried to laugh through her tears. She was absolutely overwhelmed with how things had turned around for her.

Chapter Seventeen

Once Pat had the morning dishes cleaned and everything in its place, she refilled their coffee cups. They picked up their cups along with the pot of coffee and headed out to the front porch. Randy told her he felt that he would like to make one more ride down to that ranch and scour the hills to make sure there were no other cows that had survived the Indian massacre. Pat told him that she was going with him. Randy knew he couldn't discourage her, so he said nothing to dissuade her.

Pat told Randy that she wanted to ride to the settlement to their west for supplies as well as to take care of a few other things she wanted to clear up. Randy told her that the trip to look for more cattle could wait a week or so and suggested they leave in the morning for the settlement. Pat agreed. Together they worked all day around the ranch, making sure they could handle their new responsibilities. Once satisfied that all was in order, they retired to the house for dinner, and then on out to the porch for coffee and relaxation.

Gerald A. Moriarty

After some time had passed, Randy looked over towards Pat and saw tears sliding down her cheeks. He asked her what was wrong, and she replied that they were tears of joy. She said that this was the happiest she had been in her entire life.

It was getting late, so they rose to go into the house and turn in for the night. Once inside the house, Randy closed the door, and Pat tugged at his arm. When he turned towards her, she snuggled up to him and gave him a kiss on the cheek. She whispered up to him a tearful thanks for making this all possible.

When Randy tried to return the kiss on her lips, she pulled away with a laugh, and pointed to his bedroom. She went to her own. You could hear both of them chuckling as each prepared for bed. All finally grew silent, and then the sound of soft snoring began coming from each room. Both had another great night of sleep, as all was now in order for there to be a well-running ranch. And all was well beyond either one of their wildest dreams.

Randy felt that he could now settle down to being the ranch hand that she had hired him to be. He wondered how much longer it would be before he would have to move on. He had been raised to know that everything came with a price. He wondered just how high the price would be to cause him to move on. He had truly enjoyed his time here on the ranch. His healing came quickly, and all the doctoring that Pat had been doing was now completed. She owed him nothing. He owed her his life. Only time would tell which way the wind would blow. He only hoped it would carry him in a good direction.

When morning came, it was with a sense of peace and tranquility. Randy got dressed, and then walked into the kitchen to start the morning fire and their morning meal. It wasn't but a few minutes later that Pat came into the kitchen, yawning and stretching. They greeted each other with a good morning. Randy had placed a pot of coffee on the stove and it had only finished boiling. He took down two cups and filled each with steaming hot coffee.

Randy took his cup and told Pat that he felt like sitting out on the front porch to enjoy the coffee and scan over their successes from the past few days. Pat took her cup, along with the pot of coffee, and followed Randy out the door. As they sat there with looks of satisfaction one could detect a look of pride that had crept in as well. Randy wondered aloud what his chores for the coming days would be. He had already made all the immediate repairs that needed to be done. Pat said that she would like to expand the ranch someday.

That kind of surprised Randy. She went on to say that someday someone would come along and claim all the grazing land for their own, shutting her out from raising a larger herd than she now had. Up until now, they had been free grazing on publicly owned land. Randy then realized what she was talking about and knew that she was right. He asked her if she had an idea in which direction she thought she would like to expand. She just sat there with a look of being in deep thought.

Finally she told Randy that her husband had always thought they should annex all the land between her ranch and their closest neighbor to the east. She said that would shut out that rancher from expanding his ranch in her direction. She said it was some of the best grazing land available with many good watering holes. The neighbor had as yet to use that land. Randy asked her if the settlement to the west had a government land office. She said it did. Randy told her that she should dig out the deed to her property, and take it with her to the settlement.

She rose up and said that she was going in to prepare their breakfast. After another cup of coffee, Randy stood up, picked up their cups along with the pot, and then headed in to join Pat. Once he had placed the pot back on the burner, he turned to sit down. In front of his place-setting was an envelope. He asked Pat if she planned to sit there, and she told him no, that she had placed the deed there for him to   investigate. He picked it up and slipped the deed out of the envelope to glance over it. He had not seen a deed prior to this moment.

Once he had scanned it over, he told Pat that they sure didn't make deeds easy to understand for the common person. She chuckled, as she placed a plate of pancakes and eggs in front of him. She told Randy she would have to hire a lawyer when they arrived in the settlement. She took up her plate and joined Randy at the table. They ate in silence. Once the breakfast dishes and cookware were cleaned and put in their proper place, they began putting together all they would need for the next few days until they returned.

They took all they had packed out to the barn and placed it in the buggy. Pat told Randy that there was a waterhole up in a draw just south of the ranch that had good food surrounding it. She said they should herd the cattle up to that draw and just trust that the cows would stay there until she and Randy returned. Randy agreed. For the next hour, they worked the cattle up into that draw. The cattle immediately all went to the waterhole. That was good, as they would not wander far from that waterhole now that they were aware it was there.

Once they were satisfied they had done the right thing, they went back down to the ranch. Randy asked Pat what they had paid for their ranch, and Pat said they had paid fifty cents an acre for all the land. She told him that all they would have to pay for was the land, as it was barren and unsettled. Randy headed to the house. He went in and headed to the hiding place under the chair. He retrieved the bag with his money. He took out all the paper money and placed it back in the hiding place, and then placed the rug and chair back over the door of the hiding place.

Randy brought the bag out and placed it in the compartment under the buggy seat. They climbed aboard the buggy, and Pat directed Randy to pull up against the porch. When they were up against the porch, Pat climbed down and went into the house. When she returned, she was carrying their bedrolls. Randy smiled. She smiled and pointed out to

Randy that there were two bedrolls. They whipped the horse into a gallop with both of them laughing. They wouldn't reach the settlement until late on the next day.

Chapter Eighteen

It had been a fun trip to the settlement. They took two rooms for the night. Randy thought that was a waste of money. They headed over to the eatery and settled in for a good meal. They discussed everything they needed to take care of while they were at the settlement. The first order of business would be purchasing the land. Randy felt they should explore the market for the beef for when they were ready to sell some of them. Pat said that she had a few personal matters she would like to take care of. Randy asked her what she had to take care of, and she told him it would no longer be personal if she told him, and then she rose to leave. He just sat there with a dumb look on his face.

They had arrived in the late afternoon and were too tired to do anything else. Now that their meal was consumed, they decided to head back to their rooms. Randy acted like he was going to Pat's room. She held up her hand, and then pointed to his room. He told her he had forgotten which room was his. They laughed. It would be a peaceful night of sleep.

With all they had accomplished during the past several weeks, Pat felt she would be quite happy ranching for a living. Randy was relieved that most of the stolen money would be gone after they bought the property. All he would have left to do would be to find another settlement to the north to get rid of what was left of the bills.

Morning came, and after their breakfast was behind them, they began taking care of all their needed business dealings. They found the land office and went right to work procuring a deed for the land Pat desired. After she had everything all laid out for the clerk, and the records showed the land was available, they purchased it and were astonished that they had gotten it for so little. They then decided to look at the land towards the area where they had placed the cattle. It was available clear up to the ridge above the draw, so Pat purchased that as well.

They left the land office overjoyed by all the success they had achieved. Pat told Randy that she saw no need to stay another night. She felt they had better get all the supplies they would need for the next several months. They had a lot of work ahead of them staking out all the land Pat had just purchased. They would need to build several corrals in the outlying areas of the new additions. Randy felt they would need to build a couple of line shacks.

Pat told Randy that he was too far ahead of her with his plans and would need to slow down, as they had the rest of their lives to take care of all that needed to be done. Randy felt puzzled with that statement. As they were walking towards the mercantile, Pat told Randy to go ahead and begin putting together their needed supplies, as she needed to take care of that personal business she had mentioned before. They each headed in their own direction. Pat headed directly towards a church she had spotted.

When Pat arrived at the church, she didn't hesitate one minute to shout out for the pastor. The pastor appeared from a room in the back corner of the church. He asked Pat what the nature of her business was, and Pat filled him in all that had happened since the death of her husband. After Pat had laid it all out, the pastor told her that he could see no problems with her plan and wanted to know how soon she would like to get the job done. Pat told him immediately would be great. The pastor was taken aback a bit, but agreed to it all.

Pat left the church and headed for the mercantile. Once inside, she found Randy and they tallied up all the items Randy had set aside. Pat thought of a few more items and she placed them with the others. Once satisfied that they had everything set out they would need, they made the purchase. Randy went to the stable and retrieved the horse and buggy and, after settling with the liveryman, he rode back to the mercantile. Once he arrived, he saw that Pat had all their supplies stacked up on the boardwalk in front of the mercantile. They wasted no time loading it all in the back of the buggy.

They headed to the hotel from there. They retrieved their belongings, and then settled up with the clerk. They climbed aboard the buggy, and Randy turned the buggy towards the ranch. Pat stopped Randy and told him that they had one more piece of business to take care of. She directed him to the church. When they arrived, they climbed down from the buggy and tied the horse off to the hitch rail. Pat headed on into the church. She stopped and told Randy to come with her. He entered with Pat and they were immediately met by the pastor along with another man and woman.

Pat stopped and turned towards Randy. She then reached over and turned him towards her and asked him if he would marry her. He went into shock. He stammered and stuttered for what seemed like forever. She again asked him, with a big grin on her face. She went on to say that if he wasn't going to ask her, then she would do the asking herself. The pastor and the other couple were rolling in laughter. Randy finally regained his composure and stated that he might just as well, as he didn't know where the man with the shotgun was standing. They all burst out with more laughter.

The pastor began by explaining the presence of the other couple. He told them that the couple would not only be the witnesses, but their best man and maid of honor. Randy was standing there with his face all ashen looking. His legs had begun to shake uncontrollably. The pastor directed them to walk up the aisle with him, and then he stopped them in front of the alter. After that, the other couple stood closely by their sides. The pastor began the ceremony and, once they both had said their *I Dos*, the pastor pronounced them man and wife.

Randy started to walk away, but the pastor stopped him. He told Randy that if he wasn't going to kiss the bride, he would do it for him. Randy told the pastor that Pat wouldn't let him. They all burst out with laughter. Randy took Pat in his arms and told her that he loved her. She asked him why he had waited so long to tell her that. He said that he didn't think she felt the same way. She grabbed him in her arms and laid the biggest kiss on his lips that a person ever had seen, and then she came up for air. She asked him if he was convinced now.

They thanked the pastor and the other couple and turned to leave. The pastor gave a grunt, like he was clearing his throat. When they turned to see if he was all right, they found the pastor standing there with a big grin on his face, holding out his hand. They once again burst out with a hard laughter. The pastor spoke up telling them that he had to make a living too. Randy slipped a gold piece into the pastor's hand. As they turned once again to leave, they heard another clearing of the throat and turned to see the witnesses standing there with their hands out. Randy slipped another gold coin into the man's hand and told him to split it with the woman.

They then walked out of the church and stepped aboard the buggy. The pastor and two witnesses threw rice all over them as they whipped the horse into a gallop. Randy and Pat waved goodbye as they left. Once they had reached a point where the settlement was out of sight, Randy reined the horse to a stop. Pat asked him why he had stopped. Randy told her that this would make a nice spot to camp for the night. A big grin came over each face, and then Pat stated sternly that they weren't stopping until it began to turn to dusk. Randy put on a sad face, and then whipped the horse into action once again.

Chapter Nineteen

They rode on in silence for the remainder of the day. In the late afternoon, Randy yawned and said it was getting pretty late and that they should set up camp for the night. Pat told him they could still make another couple of miles yet. Randy then put on another sad face. Pat refused to stop several more times before they finally set camp for the night. Randy unhitched the horse and tied it off to a tree. He then went to the buggy and reached in for the bedroll but found them both gone. He looked around and saw Pat standing beside both bedrolls—they had been spread out side by side.

When Randy began to say something, Pat walked over to him and placed her fingers over his mouth. She reached over, took his hand, and led him to the bedrolls. She said that one of them would make a soft bed under the other. A big grin came over his face, and he immediately began stripping off his clothes. Pat just stood there watching. He asked her what was wrong, and she said she was hungry. Randy said he was hungry too but not for food. Pat laughed and began to strip off her clothes as well.

Together they crawled under the blankets and began to hug and kiss passionately. They spent the entire night in ecstasy. Randy was the happiest man in the world at this moment. Pat was extremely happy as well.

It was late in the morning when they woke up. They lay there for quite some time before Randy finally got up and got dressed. Pat followed shortly after. Randy had a good fire going while Pat dug out the makings for breakfast. When they were done eating, they cleaned the cooking gear and packed it away in the buggy.

Pat went over, rolled up the bedrolls, and placed them in the buggy as well. Randy hitched the horse to the buggy, and they both mounted up for the ride home to their ranch. It was a joyous ride. They joked and laughed their whole way back. They arrived in the late afternoon and immediately began putting all the supplies in their proper places. Once the buggy was empty, Randy rode over to the barn and unhitched the horse. He stripped all the gear from the horse and turned it loose in the corral. You could see it was happy to be back with the other horses.

Randy stood watching the horses for a moment, and then turned to head back to the house. As he did, he felt the cold nose of a horse against the back of his neck? When he turned around, he found his horse standing there with a contented look on its face. The horse then stuck its head back over the rail and nuzzled up and down Randy's cheek. Tears came to Randy's eyes. That was the first time Randy's horse had ever shown him any affection. He stood there for quite some time scratching his horse in one place or another. It was a great relationship they had developed.

Pat called out for Randy to come have some coffee with her. He joined her on the porch. They sat in the rocking chairs looking out over the surrounding hillsides. Pat told Randy she couldn't believe that all that was visible and well beyond belonged to them. Randy mentioned that they should stake out their boundaries first thing in the morning. Pat agreed. She told Randy she wanted to ride up into the draw and see how their cattle were doing.

When the coffee was gone, they rose, and while Pat was putting the pot and cups back in the kitchen, Randy went to the corral and saddled their horses. He led them both back to the porch. Pat came out, and they mounted up for the ride. It didn't take them long to reach the base of the draw. As they rode up into the draw, they began spotting their cattle spread all over the hillside grazing away. Pat let out a sigh and told Randy that she felt much better about leaving the cattle out to free graze. The cattle had stayed up in the valley where Pat and Randy had left them.

They rode up into the draw and swung up and rode along the upper ridges back towards their ranch. They were satisfied that there was enough feed to hold the cattle for a few more days. They would drive them up into another draw after they had the new property staked out. They ended their day back at the ranch house. It was beginning to turn to dusk. After their evening meal was completed and the pots, plates, and utensils were cleaned and put in their place, they wasted no time turning in for the night.

Randy had a big grin on his face as they headed to Pat's room. He said good night, and then headed for the other bedroom. She asked him where the heck he thought he was going. He said that he was so used to being banished to the other bedroom that it had just become a habit. She told him to get his hind end back over to the other bedroom. They laughed all the way to their bedside. They undressed and retired for the night. After a little hanky-panky, they slipped off into a deep sleep. It had been a long few days taking care of all their business at the settlement. Now they could settle down to ranching.

They woke just as it was beginning to break light. After they got up and dressed, Randy got the fires going and Pat made up some pancakes, along with eggs and bacon. It would hold them until they returned from staking out their new property boundaries. After Randy had the buggy hitched up to the horse, he saddled his horse just in case they would need it. He tied it off to the rear of the buggy. He loaded all the tools they would need along with numerous stakes. He crawled up onto the buggy and rode over to the porch of the house.

Pat had set on the porch two baskets of food, the coffee pot and coffee grounds, as well as water for coffee and drinking. Randy stepped down from the buggy and loaded the baskets into the buggy. Pat then came out of the house carrying their bedroll in case they had to spend the night, which made sense to Randy. Once they were satisfied that all was in order, they headed east towards their neighbor's ranch. After a couple of hours, they

Gerald A. Moriarty

spotted cattle scattered across the range in front of them.

They continued riding east towards the other ranch. After a half hour had passed, they spotted a lone rider coming towards them. Pat recognized the man as the owner of the ranch adjacent to theirs. When they met up, they cordially greeted one and another. The rancher asked them what they were doing so far over this way. Randy explained that they had just purchased all the land between his ranch and their own and were there to stake it out. The rancher's face turned ashen. He asked them if they were going to drive his cattle off the land.

Randy told him that there was no need for that, as it would be some time before they had enough cattle to need it for grazing. Pat spoke up and said that he could continue using the graze for the foreseeable future. She went on to say that they would not charge him for it. She then asked him why he decided to graze this way, as he had never before done so. He said that the waterhole in his western graze land had dried up for some reason. He said he knew there was good water farther in this way, so he had pushed his herd over to where they are now.

The rancher asked them what prompted them to buy up all of this land. Pat jumped in again and said that they didn't want to be cut off if someone else bought this and all the land over the ridge to the south of their ranch. She said that if that happened, they would eventually be choked out of any of the free graze land and wouldn't be able to expand their herd. The rancher said that that made sense to him. The rancher then asked if he could lend a hand staking the property out. Randy told the rancher that it would sure speed up the process, as he knew where his property stakes were located.

Chapter Twenty

Randy told Pat to stay with the buggy while the rancher and he staked out the boundaries against the rancher's property. They rode off a distance and located the first stake. Randy took up a hammer and stake, and then went to where the stake was and walked over onto the rancher's property about ten feet and began driving the stake into the ground. Randy told him that he must not have been thinking and pulled the stake back up and walked over to where the rancher stood.

The rancher told Randy to give him the hammer and stake so he could place it in its proper place. Randy handed it to him, and the rancher walked about twenty feet in the other direction and pretended to be getting ready to drive the stake into the ground. Neither of them could hold a straight face and burst out loud with laughter. It would be the beginning of a good relationship between that rancher and themselves. While placing all the needed stakes, the rancher suddenly stopped and stared at Randy.

After a minute or so, Randy became unsettled and asked the rancher if he had said something wrong. The rancher smiled and told him no. He said that it had just dawned on him where he had seen Randy before. Randy looked at him with a worried look and asked him where that may have been. The rancher said he had ridden with them when they wiped out that renegade tribe of Indians. Randy let out a sigh and said that now he too could place where he had seen the rancher before. They shook hands once more. It was a relief for both of them. Randy was hoping that it wasn't somewhere along the path during his former wild lifestyle. They went on and finished the job at hand. When done, they both rode back to where Pat was waiting for them.

Pat was in the process of making up their evening meal when they arrived. She immediately invited the rancher to join them. He declined and said that he didn't want to upset the applecart with his wife, as she would be planning on his return home soon. He bid them goodbye, and then wheeled his mount towards his ranch. Randy told Pat about the incident between the rancher and him about staking out the boundary in the wrong place, and they both laughed. He then told her about both men wondering where they had seen each other before, and finally discovered that they had ridden together taking care of that renegade tribe.

Pat and Randy settled down to their meal. After they had eaten, they sat by the fire and enjoyed their coffee together. While sitting there, Pat said that she knew what worried him and they needed to find a way of remedying that problem. Randy just shook his head. Pat said that it had been bothering her a lot too. She was afraid someone would come along someday and recognize him as the famous Mad Man Randy. She went on to say that she had considered selling the ranch and moving far up into the country north of there where no one knew of them.

Randy told her that would never happen. He said that they would think it out and come up with a better solution. It was getting late and both were tired, so they spread their bedroll out in the back of the buggy. They crawled in and soon both were sound asleep. Sometime during the night Randy felt Pat stirring around. He rose up on one elbow and asked her what was bothering her. She said that she couldn't get his past out of her mind and feared he would be spotted someday. She said she didn't want to lose two husbands.

When morning came around, after a restless night, they rose up and dressed for the day. Randy built a fire while Pat put together their meal. They sat silently while eating, and then when finished, they packed for the long ride back to their ranch house. It was a quiet ride.

They arrived in the mid-afternoon. After all was put away in its proper place, they commenced taking care of the chores around the ranch. When done, they retired to the porch and sat in the rocking chairs looking out over their ranch. They were tired from all the work they had just put behind them, so they went to bed without eating.

It was somewhere around midnight when Randy woke up. He silently sat up on the edge of the bed. Pat had been lying awake and silently rose and sat beside Randy. After some time had passed, they got up and went into the kitchen. Randy built up a fire in the cook stove while Pat put together a pot of coffee. When the coffee was ready, they took the pot and two cups out onto the front porch. They were both sitting there sipping their coffee and staring out across the ranch. The bright glow of the moon was shedding its light out across the lush grassland that lay before them towards where the cattle grazed.

Pat broke the silence by telling Randy that she had a plan that might work. She said all they had to do was find a way to implement it. Randy asked her what it was. She told him that, if there was a way of convincing the sheriff that he was dead, word would spread quickly, and no one would look for him again. They again sat there in total silence. The sky was clear, and the silver glow of a moon was slowly slipping off the horizon towards the west of them. Every once in a while, a meteorite would shoot across the sky leaving a long trail behind it.

Randy spoke up and said he thought he had something figured out that might work. He said that they should ride down to where the posse had chased him towards the hillside when he had been shot up pretty badly. He said that, as bad as he had been wounded, he must have left a trail of blood for the posse to follow until it dried up on his clothes. He went on to say that, somewhere past that point, they should dig a grave and pile rocks high on top of it.

Pat asked him how they were going to prove that it was him who was buried there. Randy told her that the hat he was wearing and the gun belt he had were the same ones that he wore at that time. He said that someone would have to take them to the sheriff and tell him that they ran into his body and buried him and kept his hat and gun belt with his firearm holstered. The sheriff would recognize the hat and belt, as he had seen them at close range when he ran Randy out of the settlement on one occasion prior to his crime spree. Pat said she felt that just might work. She went on to say that she didn't think it would be a good idea to leave a grave as the sheriff might want to see it and try removing the body.

They rose and returned to bed. After both had lain back down, they were soon fast asleep once again.

When morning came, they wasted no time getting started on the south boundary line. It was turning dark when they finished that line. They were close enough to the house that they decided to head there for the night. All they had left to do was lay out the north boundary of their new addition. They had staked out the added property on the south boundary, and when they reached the west end, they had turned north and hooked up with their original property on the west side corner fence-line.

Morning was not a welcome event, as they were both tired and sore from all the work they had accomplished. Nevertheless, they ate, and then headed out to complete the north boundary of the new property. It was shortly after noon when they completed that task, and they arrived home in the late afternoon. Pat heated the coffee, and the two of them retired to the porch and sat in the rocking chairs, patting themselves on the back for accomplishing all that needed to be done to make the property legally theirs.

They were no longer small ranchers. They had a ranch that could now support several thousand head of cattle. It would take several years before they could build a herd anywhere near half that size. There were water pools in all the right places, and the graze was great. All they had to do now was brand all their cattle and make repairs as were needed. They would take care of the branding first. Randy asked Pat if she had any idea what kind of a brand she wanted. She said that she never really thought about it.

They sat silent for a time. Randy broke the silence by asking her what she thought about a brand that depicted an upside down horseshoe with a number two attached to the bottom of the right leg of the horseshoe. Pat asked him what that would be saying. He told her they would call the ranch The Lucky Two.

He went on to tell her that an upside down horseshoe attached on any building was interpreted to mean good luck. She began to smile. She jumped up and screamed her approval. She said that it was exactly how things had gone ever since the two of them had been thrown together.

Randy went on to tell her of his thoughts about erecting a high arch over the entrance to the ranch and across the top having large letters spell out, "Welcome to the Lucky Two Ranch." He suggested an upside down horseshoe on each end of the slogan. Pat loved it and asked him why he was sitting there. She told him to get up off his dead butt and get to it. They laughed. Pat suggested hanging an enlarged brand on short chains under the arch. Randy liked the idea. They decided to make a trip in the morning to the settlement to the west of them to have the blacksmith make up the brand and letters that would be needed. They would register the brand while they were there.

Chapter Twenty-One

When morning came and they had put all in order, they headed to the settlement. They arrived at mid-afternoon the next day. While Pat did the necessary shopping, Randy headed to the blacksmith shop. After explaining everything they needed, he headed back to meet Pat at the mercantile. He explained to her that they could pick up the branding iron that evening, but would have to wait until the next trip to the settlement for the rest of the material. They could at least get the branding chore out of the way. They first had to pick up the branding iron, and then get it registered. When they arrived back at the blacksmith, they were pleased to see that he already had the branding iron ready for them. They wasted no time getting it registered.

Then they headed to the eatery and sat down to a good meal. They decided to get back on the trail towards the ranch after eating. That would put them back at the ranch sometime in the late evening on the following day. There was good moon light, and they took advantage of it by riding until the light from the moon subsided. They then unhitched the buggy and tied the lead rope to one of the buggy wheels. They stripped the harness off the horse and placed a bucket with water by the wheel. Randy gave the horse a good bait of grain. They spread their bedroll out in the back of the buggy, and then turned in.

The sun was full up when they awoke. They didn't bother with a meal or coffee, which made for a good start back on the trail to the ranch. They ate jerky and biscuits and washed it down with water. That should hold them over until they arrived back home.

They arrived in the late evening. After taking care of the supplies and putting the horse and buggy away. They ate some more jerky and turned in. Breakfast would be a welcome meal. They turned in with anticipation of what the next day would bring them.

After breakfast was consumed the following morning and the pot of coffee depleted, they began the task of enlarging the corral so they would have room for all the cattle. Then they got ready for the cattle drive. They would first have to drive the cattle down out of the draw and place them in the corral. Once that was done, the branding iron would soon get a good workout. What an exciting day it would be for both Pat and Randy. The cattle chute that Randy had built would be put to good use. They mounted up and headed towards the draw where the cattle had been left to graze. When they arrived they immediately began the task of rounding up the herd. It took a little longer than they anticipated, as the cattle were scattered over a large area.

Once the herd was bunched, they wasted no time heading them down and out of the draw towards the corral. It was late in the night when they arrived back at the corral. The drive had been a tough one, as many of the cattle had tried to make a break from the herd. No time was wasted putting the horses away and then, after a quick meal, they turned in for the night. It had been a long hard day. Sleep came with a struggle, as they were overly tired. After much tossing and turning, they finally fell fast asleep.

Morning rolled around and they prepared and ate breakfast. They retired to the porch to enjoy their coffee while gazing out towards the corral and admiring their accomplishments over the past several months. It was totally unbelievable how far they had come, from Randy lying near death's door on Pat's front porch to owning, free and clear, a ranch fully stocked with a nice herd of cattle to being married "to the finest woman a man could ever have asked for," as far as Randy was concerned. Only a power greater than they could have arranged such a perfect scenario. This day would be an exciting one.

It was now time to get the branding started. Randy went over to the corral and built up a fire in the pit they had dug previously. He piled the wood high, as he wanted a nice bed of coals to place the branding iron in. After an hour had passed, Pat came strolling across the distance between the house and corral carrying their new branding iron. She had a wide grin on her face. Randy stuck the branding iron deep down into the bed of coals.

The next task was to herd a cow into the cattle chute. Once they had the first cow in the chute, they pulled the squeeze tight in place to hold the cow steady during the process of placing the branding iron against its hind quarter. Randy pulled the iron from the fire and handed it to Pat. He told Pat that he felt she should have the honor of branding the first cow. She immediately placed the red hot iron against the hide and watched as the hair burned away allowing the iron to sear their brand into the hide of the cow. The brand fit perfectly over the old one and hid it completely.

Pat stepped back with a wide grin on her face and had tears flowing down her cheeks. Randy took the iron from her and placed it back into the bed of coals. After releasing the animal from the chute, Randy turned to help herd another cow into the chute. Pat stepped in front of Randy and wrapped her arms around his neck and applied a long lingering kiss on his lips. Randy stepped back, nearly tripping into the fire. He looked at Pat for a moment and finally asked her if she wanted to go back into the house for a while. They laughed.

Another cow was squeezed into the chute. After that cow was branded and released to the outside of the corral, the next cow took her place. This process went on until the last cow had been branded. It was now time to brand the bull. There was a gate between the corral and the pen the bull was in, so they opened it and drove the bull over into the chute. This move wasn't an easy one, as the bull was much wiser and more stubborn than the cows. It dodged the chute entrance and ran to the other side of the corral each time they herded it back to the chute entrance. Once they had achieved getting the bull secured, they wasted no time placing their brand on it.

It was now time to release the bull into the herd. It would be a welcome event for the bull. Randy and Pat saddled their horses and began herding the cattle back towards a new draw where they had better grass on which to graze. There was a good spring for them located high up in the draw. It was, once again, in the middle of the night when they had accomplished the drive. They stayed with the herd most of the night to make sure they settled down from all the excitement of the day. It was a long ride back to the ranch house. Once they had the horses taken care of, they headed to the house and were removing their clothes all the way to the bedroom. When they were comfortably tucked in, they fell sound asleep.

It wasn't until late the next morning when they awoke from their sound sleep. Pat was the first to get up. Her banging around in the kitchen making their breakfast caused Randy to get up and join her. Pat placed a cup in front of Randy, and then returned to the stove. Randy sat there for a time staring at the empty cup. He then asked Pat if there was any coffee in the pot. She looked at him with a quizzical look on her face. He tipped the cup over to show her that it was empty. They both burst out laughing. She filled the cup and once the pot was back on the stove, she placed an empty plate in front of him.

He once again sat there looking down at the empty plate. She saw the look on his face and told him not to worry. She then placed a plate full of pancakes on the table along with butter and syrup. They chuckled as Pat sat down to join him. She brought the coffee pot and her cup with her. She told Randy that she would do much better once things got back to normal. He asked her what normal was. They laughed. It had been a long time since they could just do things as they had time and energy to do them. Nothing had a sense of urgency to it.

Once their bellies were full, they took their coffee to the porch and sat rocking while sipping on their coffee together. After a moment or two, Randy turned to say something to Pat and found her looking at him with tears flowing down her cheeks once again. They were tears of sheer joy. It was something she had not enjoyed before in her life. There was such a sense of peace and tranquility about her life at this time and place. She just whispered a thank you to him. He smiled, reached over, and took her hand.

They sat like that for a long time. Randy thought about his past and wondered how he ever survived to reach such joy in his life. He had no desire for the *exciting* life that he had left home to find.

Chapter Twenty-Two

With the arrival of morning came thoughts of making an end come to Mad Man Randy. Randy told Pat that his notoriety was from his fast gun and fast horse. Pat said that she had an idea of how they could get his past put behind him. She threw the idea at him about getting a rumor spread throughout the territory where he was well known that he had been killed by a gunslinger who had hunted him down and shot him in the back. Randy told her that he didn't think it would be believed, as he had not been seen anywhere throughout his known area of rampages.

She agreed. He suggested once again that they go down to the area where the posse had chased him and make a fake grave, then have someone take his hat and gun belt on down to the sheriff that led the posse and tell him that he had been found dead with his horse standing over him with massive injuries on his legs and underside that looked like it had been ridden through brush where there was no trail. That he had been shot up by someone leaving him with four bullet holes in his body. Pat said that she felt they should not make the grave as the sheriff would probably want to see it.

They mulled it over as they sipped on their coffee. Pat came up with the idea that she could take the hat and gun belt, along with his horse, down to that sheriff and tell him that her husband had found the body with the horse standing over it. That the body had multiple bullet wounds that had all appeared to have come from his backside. He was coming home from a trip down south to buy a bull when he stumbled across the body. He had told her that he had heard of a man by the name of Mad Man Randy that had been on the run down that way.

If the sheriff wanted to talk to her husband, she would tell him about his being killed in an argument with a man in the settlement to the east of where they lived. Randy said that he hated the idea of giving up the horse and belt but agreed that the idea was as sound as any they had come up with yet. He told her they shouldn't rush into it though and should think it out thoroughly before they acted on it. As they sat sipping their coffee and giving deep thought to what Pat had suggested, they both agreed that it was a feasible plan.

All they had to do now was put the plan into motion. It was decided that they would wait for a week or two so they could make sure that all was in order around the ranch. Randy would ride the extra horse and take along the extra saddle and bridle so everything that would have been found with the "dead" body would be with them to show to the sheriff.

They went on preparing the ranch for their departure. It would take them the better part of a week to complete the task before them. They would be greatly relieved if the sheriff swallowed the story. Randy would not ride into the settlement to the sheriff's office, as there was the remote possibility that the sheriff would recognize him through the beard he had grown in the meantime.

The time had come for them to make the ride south to take care of business. After placing the saddle and reigns on Randy's horse, he went through the saddle bags to make sure that the only things in them were some of Randy's personal items. Pat noticed that there still was some blood stains on the bags and saddle. She pointed that out to Randy. He was glad to see that, as that would further convince the sheriff that she was telling the truth. Randy then hung his gun belt along with the pistol over the saddle horn. Randy pointed out to Pat that there was still blood stains on the holster also. He made sure there were only empty cartridges in the chamber. He emptied the belt of most of the cartridges. He took his old hat and placed it on the saddle horn.

Then they began their trek south.

After two days, they arrived at a point where Pat and Randy had to part ways. Randy would need to remain behind. They held each other tight, kissed, and said their goodbyes. Randy had made sure they weren't within sight of where the sheriff had begun the chase after him, by approaching through a draw to the west. Following Randy's directions, Pat made the ride around the end of the mountain range where Randy's old hideout had been. She arrived at the outskirts of the settlement leading Randy's horse.

As she entered the settlement, she could hear shouts from people recognizing Mad Man Randy's horse. She spotted the sheriff's office, and rode towards it. As she was in the process of dismounting, the sheriff came rushing out and over to the horse. He turned towards Pat and demanded to know where she got that horse. Pat coldly looked the sheriff in the eyes and sternly told him to back off. That set the sheriff back a step. He wasn't used to anybody talking to him like that, let alone a woman.

He apologized and invited her into his office. She refused and told him no, as it had been a long hard ride down this way, and all she wanted was a meal and some hot coffee. She had him over a barrel as he didn't know how to reply. He told her that the eatery was across the street. He told her to come, that he would buy her a meal. He stuttered and stammered all the way into the eatery. Pat was a beautiful woman, which added to the sheriff's nervousness.

They sat at a table against the far wall. After ordering their meal, they sat enjoying their coffee while waiting for the food. Pat was in complete control of the meeting between them.

The sheriff kept trying to bring up the subject of the horse, but Pat was having fun and kept putting him off. You could see that it was irritating the sheriff, but he feared that if he insulted her, the settlement folks would turn on him. He was being extra polite with her. Nobody had ever seen him like that, and the mumbling began. As some of the folks left the eatery, you could hear laughter coming from others as they heard the story.

Their meal was served and, after it had been consumed, they sat back to enjoy their coffee. Pat leaned back and asked the sheriff what it was he wanted to talk about. That irritated the sheriff, as he knew she was aware of what he wanted to talk about. Pat couldn't hold it back any longer and burst out with laughter. She settled back and told the sheriff she was just having a little fun at his expense. She said that she was here specifically to see him about the horse and how she had come about getting it. The sheriff sat back with a smile on his face and told her that he wasn't going to live this down for a while.

Pat began right off by telling the sheriff that her late husband had been down south to buy a prize bull that he had heard about. He was returning home disappointed that he hadn't been able to meet the seller's price. He had told her that somewhere on the other side of the mountain range to the north of the settlement he discovered a body with the horse standing over it. The man had been shot up pretty bad. It appeared to her late husband that the dead man had been shot from the back as all four bullet holes he saw entered from that side. She went on to say that her husband dug a grave and buried the man's remains after removing the man's gun belt. The sheriff asked her where the grave was. She said that she wasn't with her husband as someone had to mind the ranch.

The sheriff blurted out where was her husband. She just sat there with a smile on her face. She finally asked him if he hadn't heard her say her "late" husband. The sheriff's face reddened from embarrassment and he apologized to her. She accepted his apology. She told him she would tell him everything she knew about it if he would just sit and listen. There were still some patrons sitting nearby and muffled chuckles could be heard coming from them.

Pat then went on and began filling the sheriff in all that she knew. She finished by telling the sheriff that her late, she emphasized late, husband said that he placed the gun belt over the saddle horn and was about to ride on when he spotted the man's hat a short distance away. He picked it up and brought it along as well. Her husband had heard about an outlaw by the name of Mad Man Randy that had been operating down in these parts. Her husband had told her that he was going to ride down this way one day to see if there might be a reward for the man.

The sheriff asked her why he had not done that. She again sat back with a smile on her face and told the sheriff that it would have been a miracle if her husband had been resurrected from his grave so he could have accomplished that task. The folks in the eatery burst out with laughter. The sheriff once again sat with a red face, partially out of anger. The sheriff rose and asked Pat if she would mind going with him to look the horse over. They rose and the sheriff told the waitress to put the meals on the sheriff's tab.

Chapter Twenty-Three

When they arrived back at the location where the horse had been tied off, they found a crowd standing around the horse. The sheriff ordered everyone away. As he was looking the horse over he recognized it as the one Randy had won in a poker game. He then turned his attention to the holster. He again recognized the holster, as he had once placed Randy under arrest for public disturbance and had to take his gun belt and firearm from him. The sheriff then turned his attention to the saddle. He noticed that there were still blood stains all over it. There was a lot.

He then looked at the saddlebags. He opened one and searched through it. All he found was Randy's personal belongs, such as razor and a bottle of smelly stuff that was used to make men smell good to the ladies. He went around to the other side and searched through the other bag and found it empty. He was noticeably irritated. He asked Pat where the money was. Pat said that her late, again emphasizing late, husband said he had found a hundred and fifty dollars in one of the bags and in the pockets of the dead man. The sheriff asked her where the money was, and Pat said that her late, again emphasizing late, husband had gambled it away the night he got shot and killed over a card game.

The sheriff stepped back and said that he had seen enough and was convinced that Mad Man Randy was indeed dead, as he never would have given up his gun, hat, and horse, which he had prized so much because he could get away from the posse on it. He said the last time they chased after Randy, they must have hit him pretty hard a few times, and he died from the loss of blood. The sheriff said he would have to deduct the hundred and fifty from the reward. That perked up Pat's ears a little. It meant she was going to receive the reward. She told the sheriff that it sounded fair to her. He went on to presume that this explained why he had not heard anything about Mad Man Randy for so long. He invited Pat into his office and had her sit down across from him.

He reached in his desk drawer and withdrew a form. He wrote out a draft that she was eligible to receive the reward of five thousand dollars, minus one hundred and fifty dollars squandered on poker, for bringing in proof of the demise of Mad Man Randy. He handed it to her and told her to take it to the bank and she would be given the reward in exchange for surrendering the draft. He rose up and extended his hand. They shook hands very briefly. The sheriff was glad to be rid of her.

When she reached the door, she turned and told the sheriff that the horse had been pretty badly torn up and couldn't run very well. She asked what he wanted her to do with it. The sheriff told her with a big grin on his face that the horse now belonged to her. He thought he had pulled one over on her. She just smiled and headed on over to the bank. When she had finished her business at the bank, she returned to her horses and mounted up for the ride to rejoin Randy. The sheriff was standing just outside of the jail. He told her to be mighty careful with all that money on her as there were folks who would surely like to relieve her of it.

Pat thanked the sheriff and wheeled the horses around and rode on out of the settlement. She couldn't wait to rejoin her husband at the campsite where she had left him. As she rode and topped out over a knoll where she had a good view of her surroundings, she would look around for the possibility of being followed. It was a nerve racking ride. It was beginning to darken, and the thought of having to spend the night alone in the wilderness worried her. She remembered approximately where their camp was, but had not as yet seen any sign that would direct her to it.

Pat continued riding in the direction she knew she had to go. There was only a faint sliver of light from the moon to guide her. She topped over a ridge and swung more northerly, looking for a better path to make her way. All of a sudden she saw the faint glimmer of firelight coming from deep down in the canyon below and to the north of her. She withdrew her sidearm and was about to fire a shot, when she thought that it could be a band of Indians. She replaced her sidearm in the holster and slowly picked her way towards the glow.

After another hour, she worked her way to a place where she could get a good look at the camp where the fire was. She sat there for what seemed a very long time studying the camp, looking for any movement that would tell her if it was Randy or maybe an Indian encampment. She finally let out a sigh of relief when she spotted Randy carrying an armload of firewood over to the fire's edge. She rode on down into the camp to the surprised look of Randy. She dismounted into the open arms

161

of her husband. They held each other for a long, long time. She finally looked up into the teary eyes of her husband. She too had tears flowing down her cheeks.

When they finally parted, Randy took care of the horses. He went back by the fire and poured Pat a cup of hot coffee. He then prepared a couple of steaks along with fried taters. He had a jar of carrots left, so he heated those as well. When the meal was ready, he dished her plate up and handed it to her. He then dished his own and sat down close beside her. He reached over and lifted the pot of coffee from the fire's edge and refilled their cups. After replacing the pot by the fire again, he leaned over and gave her another kiss.

When they finished their meal, they cleaned up and put everything away. They again sat near the fire's edge and enjoyed some more coffee. Randy wanted to hear all about Pat's trip into the settlement. She told him all that had happened from the time she entered the settlement till she left. They laughed many times during her retelling of the sheriff's clumsy statements. Pat rose up and walked over to where the saddle lay and retrieved the money from the saddlebag. She walked back to Randy and threw the money on the ground by his side. His eyes flew wide open. She finished telling him of the reward. Randy sat there shaking his head.

He reached down and pickled up the money and handed it back to Pat. She returned to the saddle and placed the money back into the saddlebag. Once she sat back down beside Randy, she explained that she had received the reward for bringing in proof of "his" death. She pointed her finger at Randy and said, "Bang! You're dead!" Randy sat there with a look of disbelief. She said worried all the way back carrying all that money with her. He told her that he could relate. They turned in so they could get an early start towards home in the morning.

When morning came, they immediately began their trek towards their ranch. Randy decided they would head in the direction that would take them to that rancher's place, the one who had lost his family. He wanted to check around to see if they may have missed some cattle. They arrived early the next morning. As they scouted out the hillsides surrounding the ranch, they saw no cattle. They headed towards the draw where they had found the other cattle, even though they felt they had already recovered all the cattle in the area. As they headed up into the draw near where the water hole was, they were astonished to find nine more head. They were all feeding around the water hole.

No time was wasted rounding them up and herding them down out of the draw and on towards their ranch. It would be another late night arrival. It turned out to be a longer night than they had anticipated. This herd was a little more cantankerous than those before. They constantly had to chase down those that tried to break lose. One in particular was giving them a lot of problems. What made it worse was that they only had a sliver of moonlight to work by. Randy suggested they let it go and come back another time to find it. They could then put it down and butcher it. Pat overruled him. They arrived at the ranch sometime in the mid-morning. They penned the herd and put away their horses. Once in the house and after coffee and a quick meal, they turned in.

When they woke up it was just turning to dusk. They walked out and checked on the new arrivals. After finding them doing well, they returned to the house and settled in for dinner. They were still pretty tired, so after they had their coffee, they turned in once again. They both slept hard and long. It was daylight when they rose up and had breakfast. As they were enjoying their coffee out on the front porch, they discussed what all they needed to get done that day. Randy said that the branding would take priority over everything else.

Chapter Twenty-Four

Randy built up the fire, and then placed the branding iron in the bed of coals. As Pat herded a cow into the chute and pulled the squeeze tight, Randy branded the animal. Once the nine head were branded, they saddled their mounts, rounded up the newly-branded cows, and herded them to where the rest of their herd was supposed to be. They had to go farther up in the draw to find the others, and when they did, the new cows melted right in as though they had all been together all along. Pat and Randy stayed for several hours to watch and make sure that all went well. Once they were confident that all was well, they headed back to the barn.

As they departed from the herd, Randy spotted what looked like a small grove of pine trees just below the ridge. They rode up to it and, after dismounting, Randy walked around among the trees. He returned to where Pat was standing with the horses. He told her that he found several trees that would make a great entry arch to the ranch. She was pleased to hear that. They now needed to get back to the house and take care of loose ends around the place. They would come back in the morning to retrieve the trees. If they had had an axe with them, they would have taken them then.

After they had taken care of all that needed taking care of, they settled down to their meal. They took their coffee out to the rocking chairs and sat reminiscing about all that had gone on during the past several months. Randy turned to Pat with tears in his eyes and said that he never was much for believing in miracles, but with all that had happened, it had to have been just that. Pat began sobbing. They both reached over and took hold of each other's hand. They sat there silently for a long time. The moon was aglow shinning out across the ranch. It was magnificent.

All of a sudden Pat jumped up and took off running towards the barn. Randy watched her as she disappeared through the door to the barn. He wondered what had put a burr under her rear end. A minute or so later, she came walking out of the barn holding something in her hands. When she arrived back on the porch, she tossed the money onto the table. They had completely forgotten about it. Randy just sat there looking down on the money while shaking his head back and forth. He told her he thought she had flipped out and was going wild. She walked over to him and sat down in his lap. That was the beginning of an interesting night in bed.

They rose up and Randy picked up the money, and the two of them went to where the stash cache was. Randy slid the chair to the side, and Pat pulled the rug from over the trap door. Randy lifted the lid and placed the money down beside the other. Randy told Pat that they needed to dispose of the paper money that was in there. She suggested taking the buckboard and going over to the settlement where they were having the letters made for the entryway. He agreed. They decided to leave in the morning.

After a good night of rest, they made an early start for the settlement. They arrived the following day. They went to the livery and picked up the iron work, and then headed to the mercantile. After acquiring all their needs plus a little extra that they wouldn't normally splurge on, they headed to the eatery. At each place they paid with the bills. There were only two left. Randy decided to buy another horse and a new saddle and bridle, along with several new saddle blankets. They didn't need them, but Randy had future plans that he hadn't discussed with Pat yet. Once he had those procured, they had spent all the bills plus some of their gold coins. That was a relief.

They went from there to the land office. Pat wondered what Randy was up to. When they arrived, Randy inquired about the ranch where the rancher and his family had died. The clerk said that the land had already been sold. Randy asked who had bought it. The clerk told him the name of the rancher who had died. When Randy explained to the clerk that the man and his family were dead, killed by Indians, the clerk told him that he would have to bring two witnesses to swear to the fact that the rancher and family were dead and had left no known surviving relatives. They then went back to the livery. Anything that wouldn't fit in the wagon, they loaded on the extra horse.

They left in the direction of their ranch and rode until it was too dark to proceed any farther. It had clouded up and felt like it was going to rain. They covered everything with tarps, including the animals. Randy was glad that he had picked up the extra tarps. They sure came in handy. Randy picketed the animals extra secure just in case the storm became worse than normal. After a good meal, they turned in for the night. The storm hit as promised. It was a doozy. The lightning was flashing everywhere. The thunder was deafening. The horses were jumping all over the place. It rained about an hour, and then stopped, as did the lightning and thunder. It was a relief. The air smelled sweet with freshness.

When morning arrived, they packed up and left without eating. Jerky and biscuits would suffice until they arrived home. They arrived in the dark that night. After offloading the buggy and horse, Randy secured the animals and returned to the house. The coffee was just beginning to boil. Pat had dinner cooking. Randy put the utensils along with the cups on the table. He took the pot of coffee and filled their cups. By then Pat was dishing up their plates. After placing Randy's plate on the table, she filled her own, and then sat down and joined him for their meal. They ate silently, and then, without hesitation, turned in for the night. It had been a whirlwind few days.

After a long peaceful night's sleep and breakfast was behind them, they retired to the porch to sip coffee and discuss what the day should entail. Randy told Pat that he would like to retrieve the trees for the entry arch. That's what they decided to tackle first thing.

After taking care of their daily chores, they mounted up after packing the saw and axe in the buggy. They took plenty of rope and a lunch, along with a pot of coffee that they could heat up. It was going to be a relaxing day. They tied two horses to the back of the wagon and threw in a harness for each one.

It was late in the afternoon when they arrived back at the ranch house. They went right to work cutting and fitting the logs. After cutting the two standards to hold the cross pole, they notched the top into a wedge so the top pole would sit snuggled into the top and they wouldn't have to worry about it falling off during a storm. Randy went to the shop in the barn and retrieved an auger and large hammer. He had found several long dowels that, for one reason or another, Pat's deceased husband had made. They would be perfect for securing the top pole onto the uprights.

He began auguring the holes through the top arch, and then fit it to the top of the supporting poles. Once that was in place, he placed the auger bit into the previously drilled hole and augured on down into the support poles. He then took a dowel and began driving the dowel on down through the holes. It was a tight fit. Once both sides were complete, they retired to the house for the day. It had been a fun-filled day. Pat and Randy were a real team. When their meal was behind them, they once again retired to the front porch with their coffee. They would raise the arch the next day. That was exciting for them.

When morning arrived, they went into the ritual of taking care of all the chores, and then hooked the horse up to the buggy. Randy placed a small auger bit and brace in the wagon, along with several lag screws and a wrench to screw the lags into the iron ornaments that they would install before they raised the arch. It was an exciting morning. Once Randy had the letters and brand ornament secured in their proper places, it was time to find and retrieve some rocks to set the poles on.

Once the rocks were loaded, Randy cut and threw six small poles about eight feet long into the wagon to be used as side supports. He had left them long enough to cut the ends off so he could make spikes to drive into the dirt to support the bottom of the support poles. Once back at the location of the arch, Randy placed the rocks, one on each side of the wagon trail leading into the ranch. He then trimmed the ends off the poles and cut the short pieces into a point. He trimmed the poles to fit on the side of the uprights. It was now time to raise the arch.

Chapter Twenty-Five

Pat suggested having an arch raising celebration by inviting all the neighboring ranchers and their families over for the event. The men would help raise the arch. Afterwards they would all settle down to a great day of fellowship and getting to know all the surrounding ranchers and families. It would be a potluck meal which always has a tendency to bring much joy to the events. It would be the first time that Pat had ever had the chance to get to know any of her neighbors. Her deceased husband had been a known rebel rouser, and all the ranchers did their best to avoid them.

The next two weeks were spent making the visits to all the ranchers and inviting them to the celebration. They all accepted the invitation with joy. Almost all of them said that it was well overdue that something like this came along to bring them all together. During that time, several welcome rainstorms swept the area soaking everything and filling all the waterholes along with increasing the depth of their water wells. It had been a long, hot, dry spell. Now the grass was turning green and growing everywhere. It was a joyous lead up to the celebration.

The day came for the event to begin. All arrived during mid-morning. In all there were nine families that had come. Pat and Randy hoped they had not missed inviting any ranchers. By the time they were ready to raise the arch, the women were already laying out the meal. Many had brought jugs of whisky and wine, and one of the ranchers had brought a wagon load of what he called bathtub beer. A tub was brought out and the bottles filled it up. Then he drew water from the well and filled the tub. The water was nice and cold so it made the beer taste better.

It was becoming evident that some of the ranchers were becoming overly happy, and their wives had to settle them back down by taking their drink away until after they had feasted. The men would always moan about it. As the arch began to rise, a shout of joy went out across the ranch. It was set upon the flat rocks and the support braces were set in place and nailed securely, one on each of the three outsides of the uprights. The stakes had been driven into the ground before the supports had been put in place. What a magnificent archway it turned out to be. Many of the ranchers said they would be having an archway party of their own soon.

The feast began. What a joyous time it was. Amazingly, there were no confrontations as a result of the readily available booze. Several had brought guitars and fiddles. People were dancing and singing and some were passed out from over indulging. They became the brunt of the jokes when they rejoined the others. Of course they had to partake of the hair of the dog that bit them. It would start all over again. The wives would always keep a close eye on their men as they didn't want them to make a fool of themselves. Since when did a man not make a fool of himself while drinking alcohol?

In the course of the evening, Randy discovered that seven of the ranchers were the ones who had ridden out after those Indians that had wiped out a fellow rancher's family. When Randy told them he had gathering all the cattle that had survived the slaughter and brought them back to his ranch and rebranded them with the Lucky Two brand, every one of them said they were jealous and wished they had thought of it first. Randy told them that they had inquired around as to whether there were any surviving relatives and found that there were none. One said now he knew how they had accrued such a nice herd so fast.

The men walked over to the holding pens and, while leaning on the rails, one of the ranchers asked if the bull had been with the herd when they found it. Randy said that it had been by itself deeper up in the draw. All the ranchers said it looked like a strong bull and asked if Randy would ever consider letting them use the bull from time to time. Randy told them that he didn't mind but would rather they bring their cattle to his and Pat's ranch to get them bred. They all said that they would be glad to do that. They asked Randy how much he would charge them, and he told them that he would accept one in every ten calves as payment. They all thought that was a fair deal.

It was well on towards evening when the celebration ended. It was good they had all arrived in wagons, as several of the men had to be poured into them. Randy and Pat stood out by the archway and waved goodbye to each and every one as they passed out through the archway. It had been a joyous day. All the women had cleaned up everything and left the place in better shape than when they had arrived. Pat was thankful for that. When they had all passed through the archway and disappeared from their sight on their way towards their own ranches, Pat and Randy headed back to their house and retired with coffee out on the front porch.

It had become a time of silence between Randy and Pat as they sat rocking back and forth. Every once in a while, they would hear the bawl of a cow coming down out of the canyon where they had settled in. The bull would sometimes answer the cow. They could hear an owl hooting from time to time. Coyotes were constantly howling. They were in every direction around the ranch. As long as they left the livestock alone, Pat and Randy would leave them alone. So far the coyotes fed on deer scattered all across the ranch and beyond. Rabbits were always a good treat for them too. It was a peaceful sound.

Randy got up and went into the house to retrieve a lantern as it was turning to dusk. He lit it, turned the wick down low, and then hung it on the hanger attached to the pole supporting the roof to the porch. Pat took up the coffee pot and went in and made up another pot of coffee. She returned wearing her night clothes and carrying the pot of fresh coffee. She set it on the table between herself and Randy. Randy took up the pot and refreshed both of their cups. They once again sat there in silence listening to all the noises that came forth from the night. It was a sound that spoke joy and happiness into their hearts.

Tears began to fall from Randy's eyes. They were tears of sheer joy. After some time had passed, he glanced over at Pat and saw that tears were flowing down her cheeks as well. He reached over and took her by the hand. They sat there silently for quite some time. Nothing needed to be said. They both felt the same. Randy thought he sure didn't deserve all this. He wondered why. He felt surely there must be a higher power that was watching over him. There was no other reason he could think of. The tears flowed once again.

It became quite late and the two of them retired for the night. It was a sound sleep that lasted well into the daylight of the next morning. They settled into the routine of the daily needs of running a ranch, which was up and running smoothly. The ranch prospered from time to time with the birth of each new calf as well as the calves that came in payment for the use of their bull. They had acquired another bull from one of the other ranchers that lived quite a distance up towards the north. They didn't want to get too much inbreeding, as it had a tendency to cause

179

problems with new calves being born deformed. With the new bull doing the breeding of their cows, they kept the other bull happy breeding the neighbor's cattle.

They built two line shacks, one in the middle of each of the two new parcels of land they had acquired. They knew that the time was quickly coming that they would have to hire some help to relieve them in these times of expansion. The drought was definitely over, and the grass was healthy for grazing. The water holes were overflowing once again, and small streams had formed below them. It was a dream that had come true for all the ranchers.

As Randy and Pat stood out on the front porch holding each other in their arms, once again the tears of joy formed in their eyes. They both had come through a living hell and survived. They would enjoy the remainder of their lives together in this paradise that they had been blessed with. Beauty surrounded them. Life had dealt them a bowl full of sorrow and in turn it had all turned into a gourmet of peace, beauty, and serenity. It had all begun the day hell rode in.

Randy and Pat lived the remainder of their lives in total happiness and contentment.

Review Requested:
If you loved this book, would you please provide
a review at Amazon.com?
Thank You

CPSIA information can be obtained
at www.ICGtesting.com
Printed in the USA
BVHW041832070519
547616BV00017B/494/P

9 781949 483901